# Can You Take Me There, Now?

stories

# Matthew Firth

ALLEY CAT EDITIONS

Text and page design by Patricia Cipolla @ magpie media

Canadian Cataloguing in Publication Data

Firth, Matthew, 1965 –
Can you take me there, now?

Short Stories
ISBN 1-894498-18-6

I. Title.

PS8561.I66M54 2001    C813'.54    C2001-901465-1
PR9199.3.F534M54 2001

Earlier versions of some stories have appeared in the following: *Pop Goes the Story: Canadian Fiction Anthology; Kairos 11: Female Sexuality; Trout; QWERTY; Quarry Magazine; Pottersfield Portfolio; sub-Terrain; Urban Graffiti; White Noise (UK); The Rue Bella (UK); Psychotrope (UK);* and *Fire (UK).*
They have been edited for this collection.

Boheme Press gratefully acknowledges the Canada Council for the Arts for its support of our publishing program.

The Canada Council | Le Conseil des Arts
for the Arts | du Canada

Alley Cat Editions
*an imprint of Boheme Press*
110 Elena Crescent, Suite 100B
Maple, Ontario, Canada  L6A 2J1
www.bohemeonline.com

For Andrea, again and again

## ACKNOWLEDGMENTS

Large thanks to many folks who have supported my work: my parents, Margaret and Douglas Firth; the editors of the journals, anthologies and magazines in which earlier versions of some stories have appeared; Rob Payne, Steve Shikaze, and Michelle Berry, who read earlier versions of the manuscript and offered helpful criticism; Jason Copple and Leona McCharles, my co-editors at *Front&Centre*; plus faithful friends literary and otherwise: Martin Verrall, T. Anders Carson, Kenneth J. Harvey, Mark McCawley, Michael Bryson, David Rose, rob mclennan, Hal Niedzviecki, and Kerry Schooley. Special thanks to Max Maccari and the other good people at Boheme Press who have brought this book together so efficiently. Finally, the largest thank you to Andrea and Samuel, with whom each day is full of remarkable possibility.

# Table of Contents

# CAN YOU TAKE ME THERE, NOW ?

I spent most of last night dodging cops and queers so obviously I'm not at my very best. The cops harassed me down by the harbour, glaring at me from their cruiser behind cheesy moustaches. One of the fat thugs clambered out of their car and stood over me. "What's your business here?"

He took out his nightstick: a big, inverted crucifix.

I didn't answer. I was just trying to pass the night, leaning back against a Baskin-Robbins, using the lights from inside the ice cream parlour to read *Notes of a Dirty Old Man*, but the fucking cops just wouldn't let me alone. If it had been a brick and not a book in my hand, I could have seen their point. I wasn't looking for trouble. If asked, I couldn't have said what I was looking for. I pushed on.

Up past Citadel Hill the queers became a problem. I settled on a park bench for a breather, hoping to sleep. It wasn't more than five minutes before some fucker with dyed black hair offered me twenty-five bucks to suck my cock. I was skint but not that desperate. Told the queer to make it an even fifty and he was on. He got all huffy. Sulked off somewhere to find a more willing prick. Next, some asshole was flashing his high beams at me from the curb, blinding me, keeping me from catching a few zeds. Whatever the hell he wanted I wasn't interested in waiting around to find out. I gave up on the park bench and shuffled away, back down to the town centre to find a doughnut shop, burger joint, anything all hours. Spent the rest of the night guzzling coffee at a Hortons, reading Bukowski, trying to mind my own business.

● ● ●

Eight or nine o'clock finally rolls around and I get up to take my tenth piss in the last four hours. I douse my face with lukewarm water. Blow hot air into my face. Scratch stubble and stumble back out to my cold coffee. Sit back down and ten seconds later this black guy's in my face like a shot.

"You hitchhiking?"

I look at him and recognize street crazy instantly. He's wearing the uniform: soiled greatcoat, fingerless gloves, the modern equivalent of hobnail boots. He's got on a frayed red and green toque that barely covers his head; clumps and tufts of hair jut out. I can see bits of lint in his 'fro, Christmassy, sort of. He's a month early for that.

I pause for a second longer, then answer his question.

"No, not hitchhiking. Not right now. Later, if I have to."

He sits down across from me, his scent wafting over me.

"You mind?"

"A little late to be asking," I bark, my head buzzing from all the caffeine. Then I give him a congenial nod. I can use the company.

"Name's Winston," he tells me. "Winston Whitehorse."

"Like the town up in the Yukon?"

He rolls his eyes.

"You think you're the first wise-ass to use that line on me? Yeah, like the town way the fuck up in the Yukon. Cold as fuck, as far as I know. Never been there."

He's drumming his fingers on the table madly, looking left and right, left and right.

I look at the lint in his hair.

"Sorry, I wasn't trying to be a smart ass. I've never been up there, either."

"Where you never been either?"

"The Yukon. Whitehorse."

Winston leans back and starts in again. "Right, Whitehorse. What kind of a fucking name is that for a black man? Should be Blackhorse. Got an Indian's name for fuck sakes. Look at me. Do I look like a Indian to you? A very black-assed Indian maybe."

I sip coffee and gaze around the doughnut shop. I can't tell if Winston is yelling, whispering, or speaking at a normal volume. The other customers ignore us completely. We're the only ones sitting at a table. All the others are queued up.

I look back at Winston. "Whitehorse, Blackhorse, I never thought of it that way."

"Course you haven't. We just met. Why the fuck would you've thought about my name before?"

He waggles a grubby digit in my face.

"It's like that Barry White fucker. Guy should change his name to Barry Black. That's a name for a black man."

I lean back. Rub my eyes. "Hmmn, yeah."

Winston moves in closer, giving me a stronger whiff of him. "What'd ya mean, 'Hmmn, yeah?' Makes perfect sense if you think about it. White man, white name. Black man, black name."

I do think about it for a few seconds. Then come up with, "I guess you're right. But there's always Frank Black."

Winston glares at me, sceptical, puzzled. "Frank Black? Who the fuck is Frank Black? Some dumb-assed white man?"

"Frank Black. Used to be in that band. The Pixies."

"Don't talk to me about no fucking pixies. Fuck up my head with that shit."

I wave my hands in the air. "No, no. The Pixies. Rock 'n

roll band. He's another musician, that's all. I thought it was relevant. You know, Barry White's a musician. So's Frank Black."

Winston looks at me deeply. He's mulling it over. "Maybe so," he goes. "But no one gives a rat's ass about Frank Black."

I can't argue with him there.

I look at the line-up of bored, office workers, most likely civil servants.

Winston and I fall silent for a minute.

Then Winston's on his feet, gesturing out to the street. "Let's get us something to drink before you hit the road. Get your duffel bag and I'll give you a reading somewheres."

For the first time I notice that Winston's toting a Bible in one hand. He sat down in such a flurry that I didn't notice the Good Book.

"Come on. On your feet."

I look at Winston and shrug. My mind numb from coffee, I do as instructed.

At the first stoplight he wheels around and steps back towards me. "What'd you say your name is, by the way?"

I tell him and he shifts the Bible to his left hand. I drop my duffel bag and shake his fingerless-gloved hand. The light turns green. I follow Winston across the pavement.

❖ ❖ ❖

A few blocks along my shoulder starts to ache.

"I gotta dump this bag at the train station."

Winston looks me over, sneering a little, assessing my character, something. "I thought you said you was hitch-hiking."

"Yeah, I was hitchhiking. That's how I got out here. But I'm taking a train to Montreal. Maybe thumb it back through Ontario after that. See how cold it is first."

I drop my bag onto the sidewalk and rub my sore shoulder.

"Montreal? Fuck sakes. What'd ya wanna go there for?

Full of snobby Quebec whores. They will suck your dick, though, no doubt about it."

I look at the Bible in Winston's hand.

"You read that thing or just carry it round?"

Winston's eyes alight. He holds the Bible over his head. "Don't get fucking smart with me white boy! Course I read this fucking book. All the time. Been through it dozens a times. Only book anybody oughta read."

I lug my bag back up onto my shoulder. "Just that you don't sound too religious when you go on about cocksuckers from Quebec."

Winston snorts. He follows a pace or two behind me for a moment, then races up in front and spins around. Walking backward, he wags a condemning finger in my face. "The point is, white man, I just want you to be sure that I ain't no queer, see. That's all. That's not what this is about, in case you had any funny ideas. That's why I mentioned Quebec whores."

He stabs a finger at the cover of the Bible. "Don't question my reasons. My religion. I'm a fucking priest, buddy. Don't you forget it."

He turns around again and starts walking away from me. Over his shoulder he points down a side street. "Train station's down there. Come on."

◦ ◦ ◦

This is my eighth day in Halifax. I stayed a week at the YMCA, renting a tiny room for seventy bucks. Most of my money ran out, so I spent last night on the street, knowing I had a train ticket booked for today.

I've not done a hell of a lot since I've been here. Skulked around this maritime city. Drunk coffee. Eaten cheap dinners at some Hare Krishna vegetarian place. Hung out with other bums in the public library. Ogled university women by Dalhousie. Made a couple of pilgrimages to the oceanside to stare out to sea. About what lies on the other side. Past Newfoundland, anyway. Europe. Thought about how I have no interest in seeing the shores on the other side. That's where she went, after all. Lucy. The one I'm hungup on. She of the tedious, clichéd, post-university jaunt to Europe. Train passes. Backpacks. Fucking Canadians, Americans, and Australians everywhere you look, I'd guess. All of them searching for some link to the past, full of stupid, romantic ideas. Stupid romantic students. I couldn't afford it anyway.

Lucy ended our three-year romance without batting an eye and bought a flight to Amsterdam. Probably fucked the first pot-smoking Dutchman she bumped into. Him rubbing hands greasy with mayonnaise all over her body. She sent me a couple postcards. *Such* sympathy. *Such* bullshit-we're-still-friends-aren't-we sentimentality. London. Paris. Rome. Castles. Museums. Cathedrals. Each time the cards arrived all I imagined were the cocks of different grubby Europeans fucking her. I could picture it: Lucy'd be drunk on cheap Hungarian wine. Sunbathing nude somewhere. Chatting up any prick that came her way.

I pitched the postcards, quit my job, and thumbed to Ottawa. Spent a month there doing nothing but getting pissed, drowning my sorrows.

Moved on to Montreal next. Slept on an old friend's couch. We fucked a couple times way back when. No fucking this time. So I took a Metro to Longueuil and thumbed through the rest of La Belle Province to New Brunswick, finally to where the highway stopped: Halifax, to contemplate my misery, to exercise some demons, to eventually turn around and piss off back to Ontario's fertile belly and all the sour memories that it holds.

❖   ❖   ❖

In the train station Winston scurries off to the nearest toilet. I think about dumping my bag and nipping out a side door somewhere, ridding myself of the guy. But by the time I've my duffel bag in a locker, he's back.

"Watch this and learn," he says, thumping the Bible in his right hand with his left fist.

I watch Winston work a few weary travellers. He barks quotes at them, Old Testament stuff, hard-assed passages from the Book of Leviticus, shit about who should lie with who. It doesn't get him many converts to begin with, the hard-line approach. He should back off a bit, ease into it with some Psalms and then try the fire and brimstone stuff. A couple of suits eventually relent, tossing loonies at him. Winston drops to his knees and scampers across the station's dirty floor, chasing a couple of measly bucks.

Up off his knees, he's back in my face. "Easy money. What'd I tell you?"

I look at the two one-dollar coins in his hand and shrug, unimpressed.

A minute later he approaches a couple of blue-rinse grannies. For them he reads from the Gospels, walking backward as he praises Christ. It works like a charm. Maybe he does know what he's doing. Both grannies pry crisp five-dollar bills from their purses. Winston smiles and bows, tipping an imaginary cap at them. Twelve bucks in ten minutes. Not bad work if you can get it.

Now he's back over beside me. "You dump your bag, buddy?"

"Yeah, in a locker. Train doesn't leave till three."

"Well then we got plenty of time. Clock on the wall says ten to eleven."

I look over Winston's left shoulder. He's right about the hour. But I'm growing a bit weary, a bit leery of him. I search my head for excuses to cop out, to lose him, but draw a blank.

"I got money burning a hole in my pocket. First one's on me."

Again Winston leads and again I follow.

Outside Halifax is its perpetual November grey. Winston points across the street.

"The Harbourview. Cheap beer and plenty of sluts. I'll meet you there in ten minutes. Got an errand to run first."

He hands me one of the fins.

"Buy us a couple of beers, my man."

I look at the bill.

"With a five?"

"Fuck yeah. I told you, beer's cheap at the Harbourview. And I'm a preferred customer. Mention my name and just watch the service you get."

Again he wags a finger in my face.

"Off you go. Like I said, the first one's on me."

I stand on the curb, the blue bill fluttering between my fingers in the sea breeze. Winston shuffles up the sidewalk. I think he's muttering to himself, but I can't be sure. I could use a drink. One or two beers and then that's it. Then back to the train station to catch my ride out of this damp city. Back to Montreal for a few days, then Hamilton.

◦ ◦ ◦

Inside the Harbourview Winston arrives almost exactly when he said he would. I'm sitting at a table in the virtually empty bar, nursing a bottle of Moosehead. Winston pulls out a chair opposite me and sits.

"What the fuck you buying that piss water for?"

He points at the green bottles.

"I thought this is what you drink down here."

Winston bolts forward in his chair, starts preaching again. "The fuck it is. We sell that shit to Americans and assholes like you down in Ontario. Nobody drinks Moosehead in Halifax. I hope you didn't mention my name to the bartender."

He's really worked up, genuinely upset. I ease back in my seat, keeping his breath at bay.

"No, Winston, I didn't mention your name. No harm done."

He scoffs at me and picks up the bottle. Takes a hard hit of it, emptying half the contents.

"Better get this drunk. Then you buy the next round!"

He waves the bottle in my face.

"But not this shit. Oland fucking Export my friend. That's what we drink here."

.I don't say a word. I slouch back in my chair and drink my beer. I gaze around the dimly lit bar. The usual east coast crap on display on the wood-panelled walls: ship's wheels, a couple of stuffed fish, a lobster that's probably plastic, neon beer signs (Schooner, Oland Export, Keith's; no Moosehead, I now notice).

At the front of the bar is a squat stage, a dodgy disco ball dangling from a cable. A stripper's pole stands dead centre at the front of the small stage.

I look over at Winston. He's finished his beer.

"Girls dance here?"

"What the fuck do you think that fat chick at the bar's doing here at eleven thirty in the morning on a Tuesday?"

At the bar, a large woman in a black leather mini, ratty white sweater under a black leather vest, and black fuck-me boots sucks on a butt, flipping through an *Auto Trader*.

"When you're at the bar ordering us a couple Olands, ask her what time her shift starts."

Winston swings his empty beer bottle in his hand like a pendulum, letting me know it's empty. I trot over to the bar, riffling through my wallet. I've got three tens left, plus maybe forty bucks in a chequing account that I can access from a bank machine in an emergency. But there should be no need for that till I get to Montreal tomorrow. One more beer with Winston and then I'm heading back to the train station. I got no sleep last night and could use a snooze before my train leaves.

"Two Olands," I say to the bartender.

I turn and look at the stripper beside me. She takes a long hard drag on her cigarette and ignores me. Blows a cloud of smoke out over the bar. Her lips are painted deep maroon. Her cheeks smeared in gaudy rouge. Black shit circles her eyes. I think for a minute about leaning left and feeding her my tongue, sucking on her smoky mouth and running my hands all across her lumpy, leather-clad body. I want to pull her foreign form in close to me. Stick my dick in her right there at the bar while Winston watches and applauds, offering advice like a ring-side trainer.

"Four forty," the bartender says.

I hand him a ten, my reverie interrupted. The stripper doesn't flinch, doesn't acknowledge my presence at all, even though I'm arm's length from her. I want to say something now. Get her to at least look at me. I could ask her about her act, what times she's going on. Chat her up a little. But where the fuck would that get me? Nowhere. Nowhere fast. She stubs her cigarette, squeaks off her stool, and waddles away from me. I catch a whiff of leather as she leaves.

❍ ❍ ❍

Lucy never wore leather. Apart from leather shoes, anyway. There was no way I'd ever have gotten her into a leather mini-skirt, never mind out of one. She was a conventional dresser. Proper. Sweaters, blazers, expensive jeans, the occasional long, colourful skirt. Under that, boring, bland, matching bras and panties; always pristine white. I tried once on Valentine's Day with something red and sparse. She was genuinely appalled by the panties. Called me a pervert, refused to wear them. Forty bucks pissed away that night.

The sex we had was also boring and predictable. She was boring in bed. No imagination. No sense of adventure. It got mundane pretty fast. The whole relationship got mundane pretty fast. But, for some fucking reason that escapes me now; I didn't realize it, didn't see that tedium was soon leading to a complete demise. I guess, despite my beefs now, that I was happy with the mundane, with the mediocrity.

She wanted something else, something grand. Her head was full of university crap. Not a practical bone in her body. Deluded. She talked about finishing her degree and moving to New York. What the fuck for? What was she going to do in New York City with a lousy degree in some shitty Arts programme? Didn't know a soul there. Had ideas that living in the States was her future. Then, just when all the talk about that ended, she switched to talking shit about a trip to Europe. Never once asked me if I wanted to go. What would I have said? "Yeah honey, me and you up the Eiffel

Tower, fucking eh! Just let me quit my job first." Nope. She had no plans of including me in her future. I was a footnote. A mistake. A memory.

◦   ◦   ◦

After three beers, the last two paid for by yours truly, Winston decides he wants something to eat.

"They got these great open-face sandwiches. Roast beef and a stack of mashed potatoes, peas and carrots. The works. We should get us some food if we're gonna drink all afternoon."

I look him over. I'm on the brink of exhaustion and I think he knows it, knows he can take advantage.

"I am kinda hungry."

"Let me take care of the next drink."

He reaches over and scoops up my empty, drawing it under the table.

"Told you I had an errand to run."

He flashes a mickey of rye, snickering.

"CC. Only the best for you, my friend."

Under the table Winston splashes about three fingers of rye into my empty bottle of Olands. He smiles, devious, mischievous. Then fills his bottle about halfway.

I rub my chin and look around the bar. We're still the only ones here. The bartender is watching TV, oblivious to us. I don't know where the stripper went.

"They serve food in this place?"

"The best. And cheap, too. Come on, spring for it. Three ninety-five for a big plate of hot food."

I take a sip of the rye, diluted with the dregs of my beer. I lean back and rub my stomach. Then reach for my wallet. I take one of the tens out and head to the bar. I have to call to the bartender to get him to stop watching TV for a minute. He looks at me and reaches into the fridge for two more Olands.

"No. No more beer. We wanna get some food. You got open-faced roast beef sandwiches?"

The bartender grunts and steps over to the till. He rings in $7.90 and I hand him the ten, collecting all of the change. He scoffs at me and traipses behind the bar. I look up at the TV. Phil Donahue pushes his glasses up the bridge of his nose and thrusts a microphone into someone's face. Someone somewhere offers their opinion on something. It doesn't interest me. I don't care about their problems. I've got plenty of my own problems to deal with up here.

❖ ❖ ❖

Halfway through our meal the stripper reappears. She's changed out of the leathers and is now decked out in a slutty red number. Frilly. Folds of fat droop out from her tight panties and bra. A little drunk, I start to applaud as soon as she steps onto the stage, trying to whoop but my mouth's full of mashed potatoes.

"Take it easy," Winston says. "You're acting like you've never seen a dancer before. Fuck sakes."

The stripper nods at the bartender and he slaps in some music: The Cars, from their first album. I recognize the guitar. *Let the Good Times Roll.* It reminds me of high school. She's probably about the same age as me. Probably loved this album when it came out. She gets up on the small stage and starts strutting around, trying to dance, trying to look marginally interested in what she's doing. She jiggles everywhere. But I'm loving every minute of it. I want to move closer, get right down in pervert's row and concentrate long and hard on what she's doing. But I don't. Instead, I push the remains of my lunch aside and sit back and watch her flaunt her stuff from a comfortable distance.

During the second song, a slower tune I don't know, Winston turns to me.

"You like white girls, then?"

"I'm not that fussy one way or the other."

He's looking a little restless now, distracted.

"You wanna go meet a black girl? I know one that'll fuck you this afternoon."

I look at the stripper. She's down to her panties. Rubbing her big tits. Jamming them against herself. Making the shape of an egg with her mouth.

"I got a train to catch Winston."

He looks me over, unbelieving. "I'm talking about getting you laid!"

He flashes the mickey of rye and offers me a drink. The bottle's almost empty. I look back at the stripper. She turns to show us the thong running up the crack of her ass. She bends over. Pulls on the thin strip of fabric. It bisects her flesh perfectly, symmetrically. She looks back over her shoulder, pouting, a classic pose. It does something for me, to me.

"Where we gotta go for this?"

"Not far. We got time."

I look back at the stripper. She smiles at me, I'm certain of it, even at this distance.

"What's the catch? You her pimp or something?"

Winston leans forward towards me, his back to the stripper. His plate is empty. His beer bottle is empty. His Bible sits on the table to his left.

"No, nothing like that at all. She's a good girl. Just needs it a lot. And she likes white boys, that's all. No catch. Nothing."

I'm drunk now, no question. I look back up at the stripper. The music has gone off. She's still in just her panties, bending over, collecting her belongings, her tits hanging from her like bags of wet cement. She stands up straight and gives me a smug look. I applaud again. Then raise my beer bottle to my lips and face Winston.

"Can you take me there, now?"

◊ ◊ ◊

I stumble along the sidewalk, my eyes adjusting slowly to the natural light outside the Harbourview. Winston's half a step ahead of me, leading as usual. A light drizzle falls from the sky.

"How far we gotta walk?"

Winston looks back over his shoulder and sort of laughs.

"Not far. Not far at all."

He leads me on to Robie Street. After one block, I stop in an alleyway to take a piss. I lean one hand against the red brick of a building. I tilt my head back. Drizzle sprays my face. Winston talks to me from the street.

"You got any cash left?"

I look heavenward, his voice drifting over me.

"We should get us something to drink. Something to take to Wanda. That's her name: Wanda. A bottle. A token of our appreciation, your appreciation."

I finish pissing and walk back out to the street.

"You said no catch."

"This is no catch. I'm talking about simple manners here. Remember, she'll fuck you as sure as the day is long."

I've got ten dollars and some change left.

"There's a liquor store along here."

He points down the street. I stuff my hands into my pockets and start walking.

"Now, how's about that reading?"

I look over at Winston. I erupt in laughter. I am drunk in the early afternoon. I got absolutely no sleep last night. I have spent several hours with this stranger, getting drunk, listening to his bullshit, and now I am letting him take me to see some woman who, he assures me, will fuck me this afternoon before my train leaves. It's all a bit much, too much. I toss my head back as far as it will go, opening my mouth wide and roar with laughter.

Winston is unbothered by my outburst. He ignores my laughter and reads his Bible aloud. He reads from Samuel about David's reign: "Once again the Israelites felt the Lord's anger."

I want to tell him about my anger but I'm too busy laughing. The thought makes me laugh even more. My anger. That's a joke. A damned good one.

Lucy was religious. She had faith. But not in me. Who can blame her? I seem to lack free will, direction, vision, certainty.

◦ ◦ ◦

We stop at the liquor store and I spend most of my remaining money on a bottle of red wine. Winston takes it from me on the street.

"I thought it was for Wanda?"

He looks me up and down. He pulls a Swiss Army knife from his pocket and pries open the bottle. Drinks. Offers it to me.

"Wanda don't drink."

I laugh and jingle a few coins in my pocket. It's all the money I've got left in the world until I get my hands on the forty bucks in my chequing account.

◦ ◦ ◦

Wanda isn't black. Winston introduces us, straight-faced, as if nothing is wrong.

"This is Wanda. Who I was telling you about."

I shake her dewy hand. We're inside a religious bookstore. Wanda is a clerk. She is tall and blonde, gaunt, and withdrawn. She's wearing proper clothes. Like Lucy. Some kind of dull, brown, skirt-cardigan combo. Beige blouse. Under it all—I'd wager—pristine white panties and bra.

"He's here for the group?"

Winston nods.

I'm confused now. Winston holds the empty wine bottle out for Wanda.

"We had the communion wine already."

She tut-tuts and walks to the front of the store, locking us in. Winston steps over to a curtain at the back of the store and opens it, revealing a small chapel: Christ's image in neon on the wall. I want to laugh some more but I'm too tired, completely exhausted, defenceless. He gestures with his head and I step behind the curtain. Wanda follows a minute later. She lights candles that form a circle around a crucifix six inches tall sitting dead centre on a small altar. Winston sits on a fold-out chair. I inspect the small room, chock full of Christian bric-a-brac.

Wanda leads us in prayer. I find myself down on my knees, hands folded in supplication in front of my chest, listening to her speak. Her voice rises and falls, lilts occasionally. It is beautiful. It is soothing, soporific.

Winston sits on his chair behind us, snoring. I reach out and take Wanda's hand in mine. Lean forward, pull her towards me. She smiles. I kiss her. She holds her pursed lips against mine, resisting me, my advances; not giving me what I want. I'm imagining that she's Lucy with all my might.

She rises up off her knees.

"Lucy?"

"That's not what we're here for. We're here for Jesus."

Her face is flushed red. Some colour, finally.

"Lucy?"

"Winston? Winston, who is this friend of yours?"

She's on her feet now, straightening the pleats in her skirt, brushing away something invisible.

"Lucy?"

"He come on to you? This fucker come on to you in the house of the Lord?"

I look over at Winston. I can't tell if he's serious or not. He rises out of his chair and blunders out through the curtain, drunk.

"Cast him out, then. Cast him out. CAST THE MOTH-ERFUCKER OUT!"

In the other room, I can hear him fucking with the cash register, pounding on the keys. She steps through the curtain to check out the commotion. I look around. Christ's eyes blaze right through me. I snuff a couple candles, grab the crucifix in my left fist. For some reason, I attempt the sign of the cross, messing up the order, then kick through the curtain, back into the store.

Winston is laughing, holding a palm-full of blue and purple

bills in the air, like he's keeping candy from a kid. She is close to tears, disconsolate. I'm not sure; I think she might still be praying. She seems to be muttering something. I step towards her armed with Christ's likeness on a cross. From the back, she looks just like Lucy. Upright. Proper. Pristine. Pure. Everything I can't stand.

I raise the crucifix in the air. To my left, Winston blurts something but I'm not hearing him now. I've listened to too much of his bullshit today. Wanda turns to face me and I catch her across the top of her right eye with the cross. Her flesh opens, blood all across her forehead and nose. She crumbles to the floor like a detonated building, rolls and settles, staring up at her assailant with glassy eyes. I look at the damage I have done. The welt swells. She's got a mouse above her eye like she's gone twelve rounds with George Chuvalo. Blood on the carpet. Not a peep, not a prayer, from her.

"Lucy?"

Winston looks over at me. He's in some kind of shock. He can't speak. There's blood splashed on his greatcoat, more in his hair, shimmering with the lint. I squat over her, check if she's breathing, check for a pulse.

I bunch up the sleeve of my shirt in my fist and wipe blood from her brow. Then swipe a finger across her nose, smearing blood on my trousers. I look at Winston. He jams the cash in his pocket and sprints out the door. I lean over her and kiss her lily lips. Then stuff the weapon in my pocket and chase after my witness.

◊ ◊ ◊

Back in the centre of Halifax, a few blocks from the train station, Winston turns to me. "I told you she'd fuck you, didn't I?"

He's in denial about the assault.

"Winston," I start and then stop.

"Let's get us a drink. Celebrate your fucking," he sputters, drooling a little.

"My train."

I point vaguely in the direction of the station.

"You've missed it and you owe me a drink."

I look at a digital clock above a bank. 2:38.

"No, no time. Tell you what. Take the cross. Pawn it. Buy yourself a bottle on me."

I put the bloody crucifix in his hand. He wraps his fingerless glove around it. Then stares at me. He holds the Bible in his right hand and extends his left arm in my direction, pointing the cross at me.

"Sinner, leave."

I take his advice. I bolt across the wet pavement, ignoring honks. It's all downhill to the station. I get my duffel bag from the locker. Take my seat in coach class. My mind draws a blank; no thoughts now.

I start to nod off as the train jerks into motion. Grey rain spatters the grubby window. Someone nudges my shoulder roughly.

"Ticket, please."

I lean right, give it to him, then settle again.

## MINIMUM WAGE

About four hours into my Thursday night shift Roger stops in to buy some smokes.

"What're you up to tonight?" I ask him.

He hands me a crumpled ten and I ring in the sale. I give him his change.

"Getting something to eat at Harvest Burger. After that, who knows? A few beers down the Bayview. See what's up."

He tears the cellophane off the cigarettes and leaves it on the counter. He picks up a tube of Rolos—part of some new promotion—from beside the lighters and Tic-Tacs and looks at me inquisitively. I nod and he stuffs the chocolate into his pocket. He puts a butt in his mouth. Fumbles for matches and then takes a pack from a box next to the Rolos. He tosses a nickel into the box. I wave a hand in his face when he strikes a match.

"Take it outside. I gotta draw the line somewhere. There's a by-law."

Roger snorts, extinguishing the flame with a flick of his wrist. He pivots on his boot heel and strides towards the store's front door.

"Come by the Bayview later for a drink if you want," he says over his shoulder.

I don't reply. I pick the cigarette wrapper up off the counter and toss it in the garbage. I hear the door bang closed at the front of the store. I settle back on my stool, looking blankly around the store. It's ten minutes to eight. I'm almost halfway through my shift.

I've been working at Victor's Variety Store for more than a year. I work the afternoon shift, closing the store at midnight. A woman named Sonia handles the day shift, along with the store manager, Mrs. Watowski. A continuously revolving pair of students take the weekend shifts. No one ever seems to last more than two months before a different student appears, optimistic, until they get a dose of the weekend drunks and bums that stumble in here. I've filled in occasionally on the weekends, to make a few extra bucks. I've come to know most of the drunks and bums on a first-name basis.

I'm paid minimum wage: $6.70. Before taxes, that works out to $268.00 a week, just over a grand a month. After taxes? Well, never mind that. It's likely below the poverty line, if I knew what the poverty line was. Either way, it's not nearly enough.

On top of the shitty wages I'm forced to wear a puke-green polyester smock over my T-shirt with "Victor's Variety" emblazoned on the left breast, the letters written like lightning bolts. Store policy. I asked Mrs. Watowski one day; there is no Victor. She has no idea where the store's name came from.

A couple minutes after Roger leaves, I get up off my stool and look out onto the street. It's the middle of winter. The street is dead calm. Few cars. Fewer pedestrians. Snow is piled high in grey banks by the sides of the road. Parking meters break the surface of the snow like tombstones. Light flurries fall from the sky. I can see the snowflakes in the dim light cast by the streetlights. The night sky is a blank, black slate, starless in the city.

Victor's Variety is located on the ground floor of a senior citizen's apartment building. It's part of a mini-mall that provides necessary services for the old folks who live above, shops and restaurants right in the building so they don't have to wander out into the dark and the snow to buy their milk and cigarettes. There's a dry cleaner across the corridor from the variety store. A pharmacy next to it. Wilma's Restaurant is adjacent the pharmacy. And for some reason, a karate studio next door to Wilma's.

The variety store is also situated right on the cusp of the city centre, in a lousy neighbourhood of decrepit duplexes and high rise apartment buildings built in the 1960s. As a result, the clientele at the store is mixed: mostly drunks from the nearby bars in Hess Village and old timers in their slippers and housecoats from the flats above. But it's not really a bad job, apart from the terrible pay. I'm not expected to do much: ring the sales through; keep the milk and eggs stocked up; face up the items on the shelves; mop the floor at the end of the night; make sure no one steals anything. I tend to bend the last rule.

Roger, for example, gets handouts. We have an understanding. I buy my dope from him at a decent price and I let him help himself to chocolate bars and bags of chips, entire packages of cookies if he wants. The scheme has yet to be revealed in the inventory. Not that Mrs. Watowski is too sharp on that front. She does inventory once every two months, tops. I'm not really sure what she does all day. When I take over from Sonia, half the time Mrs. Watowski has already fucked off for the day. I guess she orders the stock and sees that we get paid. Not much else.

As an employee of Victor's Variety I'm entitled to a ten per cent discount on all items in the store. Big fucking deal. I'm supposed to record whatever I eat in a ledger under the counter. At the end of the month my tab is totalled, minus the ten per cent. Whatever I owe comes straight out of my paycheque. To make it look legitimate I mark a few things in the ledger—about every fifth item or so. Of late I've made it a habit not to eat at home before coming to work. When the old fucks from upstairs stop harassing me, usually about seven o'clock—when they're all ready for bed—I begin my feast. I've had a thing for microwave ham and cheese sandwiches lately. I eat three or four a night, plus a big bag of Ruffles chips: all-dressed or salt and vinegar. Then maybe a Joe Louis or a Mars Bar. Some ice cream, even in winter. Occasionally a microwave hotdog. And I wash it all down with a litre of chocolate milk. I snack through the shift as well: Snickers, four packs of oatmeal cookies, a muffin or two, depending on how stale they are from the morning. I'm putting on weight. My complexion is suffering. But I'm also saving on groceries and Mrs. Watowski seems none the wiser.

I've also taken to sifting a few bucks from the till. You might think this isn't possible with electronic cash registers these days. Here's how it's done: A dozen times a night—maybe more, maybe less—when someone comes to the counter with a single item purchase, something familiar, like a litre of milk or a big bottle of Coke, I just hit the "No Sale" key instead of ringing in the sale and the register pops open. I compute the change in my head and plop their cash in the machine. At the end of the night when I do up the cash, I pocket whatever I come out ahead, usually fifteen or twenty bucks. Dishonest? Sure, but I consider it compensation for the shitty pay and for having to wear the ridiculous Victor's Variety smock all night. For the time being, the scam is working to a T.

* * *

Just passed nine o'clock and I'm starting to get restless. I've been playing with the radio, fingering the knobs on the old machine, trying to pick up a station from Toronto. It's not coming through clearly. I shut off the radio and pace around the store. So I can get out as quickly after midnight as possible, I spend fifteen minutes facing-up items on the store shelves. I grow bored of this; it feels too much like work. I stroll back behind the counter. I look out the front window. It's snowing harder now, a fresh cover draping the ugly streets.

Above the batteries and the packets of film on the wall behind me the skin mags are tucked out of harm's way. There's also a regular magazine rack on the store's far wall. When I was a kid the porno mags were out on display, next to the sports magazines. Now, no one wants to corrupt the young by having *Swank* and *Penthouse Forum* within sight. Seems to me the strategy isn't working.

I stand and take a copy of *Hustler* down and set it on my lap, below the level of the counter. I flip lazily through the pages. Artificially enhanced women, puckers exaggerated, painted fingers probing their own flesh, gawk out from the pages. One scene has a woman dressed as a nurse disrobing with a man. He's got his face jammed into her crotch in one shot, his eyes closed, tongue lagging like a dog. She looks thrilled with it, head thrown back, tits distended, one hand on the back of his head. But it bores me. I flip to the back and check out the advertisements: all the world's lewdest desires satisfied vicariously via the telephone. Does anyone really lick anyone else's boot heels or just talk about it to some slut who's likely not being paid much more than me?

I put the *Hustler* away; the images of the women are just a tad too raunchy for my taste tonight. I scoop *Penthouse* out of its slot. This is more like it. Air brushed photography. Pubic hair finely quaffed. Facial expressions just the right blend of naughty and nice. The third photo spread draws me in: a curly-haired brunette stripping down after a trip to the gym and then flouncing around in the shower, water beading on her perfect flesh. It makes me hard. I gaze around the store. Still no customers, haven't been for fifteen minutes now. I shift my cock over to the left, hiding the bulge with the lower flaps of my Victor's Variety smock. I take a piece of paper with "Back in Five Minutes" scrawled on it in black marker. I lock the street-side door and tape the sign to the glass. I slide the door to the mini-mall closed as well and then skulk to the back of the store to the toilet, porn in hand.

Not surprisingly, I am back in five minutes. My right hand reeks of liquid soap, the over-priced brand the store sells. I unlock the doors, making sure no one is lingering outside. I stroll back behind the counter, returning this month's *Penthouse* to its concealed slot above me and resume fingering the radio.

❖ ❖ ❖

About ten thirty, which is odd in and of itself, an old timer peeks into the store: an old woman in a ratty, long, winter coat. She makes eye contact with me and then slowly walks to the back of the store to check out the fridges full of dairy products. I stay seated on my stool, munching an Eatmore. There are mirrors positioned throughout the store so that I can observe the customers with relative discretion. This usually means following every movement made by the kids who come in here after school. And the drunks. Some of them have no fear and I've had to rifle the pockets of a few in the past, making them cough up tins of sardines, small frozen pizzas, entire loaves of bread, you name it. But the old fucks usually aren't much bother. But I'm bored as usual so I keep an eye on the ancient dame in the stained winter coat.

My suspicions prove accurate. It must have something to do with her coming in at this hour, way past her bedtime. I watch in the overhead mirrors as she slips a package of processed cheese slices into her coat. Then she grabs a pack of luncheon meat and steals it away in a side pocket. She pauses for a second and then it's off to a rack of baked goods. She stands, casually inspecting the fare. I look at her sideways this time, letting her think she's got me beat. Sure enough she slides a six pack of doughnuts under her coat, nuzzled in next to the cheese. After this she turns and slouches towards the beverages. Having her marked, I know her game. To make it look legitimate she makes a fuss about taking a litre bottle of Canada Dry ginger ale down off the shelf. She walks around with it in front of her, like it's the Olympic Torch or something. If I was a kind-hearted man, I'd intervene at this point and give her a chance to put an end to the inevitable humiliation that lies in wait. But I am not a kind-hearted man. I let her accumulate at least half a dozen items under her bulging coat without a word from me. I play stupid instead, looking distracted by the radio.

When the old bag comes to the counter with her pathetic bottle of ginger ale, I stand with my arms folded across my chest. She plunks her purchase down on the counter as if it weighs a tonne. She's trying not to move, trying to keep her booty from spilling out of her coat. I don't move a muscle to ring in the bottle of pop. The old woman fingers a squalid change purse for silver and coppers. She looks at me through the grubby lenses of her glasses. A grin begins to eat away at the corners of my mouth.

"That'll be all then, Mam?"

She plops a few coins down on the counter, preparing to sort out her payment.

"Nothing else tonight, then, eh?" I step a little closer to her.

The old woman fidgets and doesn't say a word. Probably playing deaf. She looks up at me, eyes imploring, searching my face for a glimmer of understanding, compassion, perhaps. But there is nothing on my face but a look of arrogance. I lean forward and tug at the belt of her coat. The old woman is slow, not dextrous at all. Before she can react, the lifted goods tumble out from within, crashing to the floor at her feet. I don't say a word. I glare at the old cootster: a look that suggests I'm about to scold her. But then my façade breaks and I erupt into laughter. The old woman claws at the belt on her coat. I swipe her coins away from the counter, littering them across the store's floor. The old woman steps away, confused, terrified. I hold the bottle of Canada Dry aloft.

"This all you'll have tonight?"

I chant it at her, scaring her further. She retreats out of the store, her dignity crumbled around her. I follow her, a pace or two behind, waving the pop bottle after her. When she steps out into the corridor of the mini-mall I let her get ten or twelve metres away before crouching low and bowling the plastic ginger ale bottle towards her. It doesn't roll true, veering to one side, bouncing off the closed glass door of the dry cleaner. I cackle at the sight of the old soul staggering away, groping for the button to start the elevator to carry her to her apartment above.

"Come again. Come again." I bark it a dozen times and then return to the store.

Inside I pick up the littered goods from the floor in front of the counter. I toss them in the garbage, some of the packaging damaged, the others just for the hell of it. I pick up a couple of quarters from off the floor. I pocket these and then skulk back behind the counter. The radio still isn't coming in clearly. I look at my watch. One hour to go. Another $6.70 yet to earn.

◊ ◊ ◊

Between eleven and eleven thirty I only have two customers. Neither of them tries to steal anything. I look at them sombrely and make their change, not uttering a word.

I've been eating like a pig all night and my stomach is rumbling in a bit of an uproar. At quarter to twelve I quickly race around the store, resisting nausea, facing-up a few items and topping up the milk supply. By five to twelve I've got the floor mopped, the linoleum smeared with grey water. Two minutes to twelve and I lock up the store. I run back behind the counter and punch in the combination of keys on the register to compute the night's total sales. I crank up the sound on the staticy radio. I take the float out of the till and compare the register's total to the cash left in the till. I come out just over seventeen bucks ahead. I grab a ten and a five and two one-dollar coins and then bag the big bills, stuffing them into the safe along with the night's receipt.

Above the till, just above its concealing slot, the eyes of some hotty on the cover of *Playboy* gaze at me longingly. I think for a second about taking the mag home for a tug in the morning and then dismiss the idea. I tear the puke-green smock off and toss it on my hook next to the register. I haul on my winter coat, grab an Oh Henry!, dim the lights and head out the door.

As I trudge through the new snow I can't stop thinking about the old kleptomaniac. I probably shouldn't have been so hard on her. She looked desperate, disconsolate. She's probably barely surviving on her Canada Pension. Probably eats wieners and beans every night of the week, her eyes weltering with tears as she watches *Wheel of Fortune* on a black and white TV. No relatives. A husband who fucked off long ago, maybe. Just a crappy, rent-controlled apartment in a crumbling building. I had the chance to give her a break. Make her day and all that.

I finger the coins in my pocket, some of them the old woman's quarters from her change purse. Maybe I'll make it up to her if she comes back tomorrow, slip her a care package. Maybe even enter the items in the ledger and pay for it myself, straight out of my wages. A gesture of kindness towards a shrivelled old woman. Or not. I mean, why bother? She likely won't be back. And she's not my fucking grandmother. Not my fucking responsibility. I mean, fuck her; cheeky old broad has the nerve to try and steal shit right before my eyes. Takes me for a fool, she does. Piss on her and her neighbours. If I ever see her again, I'll call the fucking cops, report her to Mrs. Watowski, get her banned for life from Victor's Variety.

I decide I can do without Roger's company. With the new snow I don't feel like slogging it down to the Bayview. I duck into the Regal instead. It stinks of spilled beer and a faint odour of piss just a pace inside the door.

I kick snow off my boots. Country music screeches from old speakers. A couple of beefy boys and busty babes prowl around the solitary pool table on my right. A few barflies prop up the bar. An old slut—too cold on the street to earn her dough—is anchored at the near-end of the bar, right next to the cash register. She looks me over, assessing my drink-buying capacity. She smiles, her teeth stained, her lips pasty. I resist the urge to laugh and ignore her instead, bellying up to the bar. I order a shot of rye and a bottle of 50. The barman's distracted by the old broad. She's cooing in his ear as he makes change. He's got an apron on. No logo, unlike mine at the store. Just a plain white smock, almost dignified looking. I lean forward and check him for a hard on. He pays me no mind. He's looking the old slut over as he pulls money out of the till. I gave him a ten. He gives me a ten, two one dollar coins and two quarters for change. The stupid fuck's got it all wrong. Thinks I gave him a twenty. What's wrong with this idiot? How much are they paying him to fuck up like this? He can't work the register worth salt. But I don't correct his error. I leave the quarters for a tip. I've come out ahead again. I nod at the poor bastard and grab my drinks.

I retreat to a table in the corner of the Regal, my back to the wall. I sup my drinks, alternating between the rye and the beer, gazing at the television above the bar. Can't hear a thing. Looks like an old episode of *The Beachcombers*, of all things. I shrug and drink. Raise my glass to Nick and Jesse, the two of them fucking around on a beach in B.C., wary of Relic. I glance over at the bartender. He's yammering away with the hooker. Probably giving her a few off the cuff, hoping the favour will be returned later. Dumb prick. My eyes wander back to the television. Beautiful British Columbia, as it says on their licence plates. Trees. Mountains. Fresh air. Three time zones away. Nothing like that around here. Hamilton mountain doesn't quite cut it. But tomorrow's Friday. One more work day, then the weekend. Thank Christ for small miracles.

# ORGASM

"Here we go again. Gin and tonic."

He sets the drink down on the table in front of her. Kicks out the leg on his stool and squats, pint in hand.

"Bottom's up."

He bobs his head and leans in close. Looks at her glass. Implores her with his eyes to drink. She slouches forward, takes up the glass and puts it to her lips. He smiles through a cigarette. Leans back, brushing greasy hair off his shoulders. Then hunkers down over his pint and knocks it back. She looks around the bar, head awash in alcohol. She drains her drink, swallows hard, and laughs a sloppy laugh, her lips the colour of blood.

"Let's get the fuck outta here, then. Get some fresh air. Come on."

He stands as he says it, pushing his stool back, knocking it over. It lies on its side on the worn, beer-soaked carpet.

She gathers up her belongings: bag, scarf, coat, gloves, hat. He waits impatiently. Cigarette dangles. He scans the room. Recognizes a few faces. Other drunks, ageing adolescents like himself.

"Come on. Let's go."

She blunders out from behind the table, knocking her stool over. It lies on its side on the worn, beer-soaked carpet.

He met her on his way to the washroom. Literally bumped into her in the corridor.

"You kill that with your bare hands or what?" he asked, pointing at her leopard-skin coat.

She didn't get the joke but laughed anyway. She leaned to her right, supporting herself against the wall.

They made small talk. She laughed and laughed, her eyes roving across the narrow frame of his body.

He had to piss.

"Wait here. Keep holding up that wall."

She laughed again and he leaned in close to her, ruffling the fake fur on the collar of her coat with his left hand, wrapping his right arm around her waist. He made something that resembled a growling sound in her ear and scooted off to piss, his cock semi hard.

It's the dead of winter. Minus ten, fifteen degrees. Grey city snow clogs the gutters, the street, the sidewalk.

He turns his collar up. Walks on ahead of her briskly. Hunkers down. Chin to chest.

She slides across the iced pavement, fat heels providing little traction. Her bag bounces off her left hip.

"Can ya wait just a fuckin' second?!"

He spins at the corner and catches her arm, steering her into an alleyway. They emerge from the blackness on the other side: a shitty, old, downtown neighbourhood. Across the street a solitary streetlight casts shadows in a park. He takes her there. Guides her into a darkened corner at the edge of a snow-covered basketball court, where out-of-bounds meets a concrete abutment. Pulls her in close. Their breath fogs.

He just wanted to come in out of the cold. Have a couple of drinks and then make his way back to his decrepit flat around the corner, piss away the rest of the night.

She was out for a night on the town with friends from way back. They swapped stories, comforted each other with familiar anecdotes, shared criticisms, bitterness.

"You remember Sheilah?" she slurred. "Ran into her down on the market. Divorced for a second time. Fuckin' bitch. Serves her right."

They cackled around the table. Painted lips bowed to meet glasses. They all got good and drunk. Started to gaze about the bar: hungry for something.

She took three trips to the toilet before she finally timed it right, loitering in the corridor just long enough to present herself to him, as if purely by chance, catching him all unawares.


They pant like dogs in the cold air. He reaches inside her coat. Paws at her tits under her sweater.

"Fuck sakes. Your hands!"

She cringes for a second, pulling away.

"Take it easy."

He laughs and glides ice-cold knuckles across her belly. She starts to protest further, then decides that this is what she wants tonight. Their faces mash together. They warm each other up. His cock fattens in his trousers.

"It must be your animal magnetism," he says, referring again to her coat.

She just purrs.

He takes half a step back and opens his pants. His dick springs out. Steams in the cold, night air. He glances quickly around the barren playground. Then pushes her head down. She goes down to her knees, bracing herself in the snow and the ice.

They had very little to talk about. He bought her drinks, five, six, seven of them in two hours, until his wallet ran dry. She knocked them all back, outpacing him. He watched her get pissed.

"Thirsty there," he said a couple of times, returning from the washroom to yet another empty glass. He lit a cigarette, contemplated her features.

She nodded her head in agreement. Checked her makeup in her hand mirror when he was at the bar. Wet her lips with her tongue. Dabbed drunken fingers at the black goo around her eyes. Smiled to herself in the small mirror, pleased with her tiny image.

"Here's another then."

He set the glass down on the table without a sound.


She makes slurping noises as she sucks him off. Holds his nuts in her right fist. Tugs at the base of his cock with her left. She's seen it done this way in pornographic movies.

She gets it done quickly. He comes and pushes hard into her mouth. She grunts, does her best to swallow. His dick steams more, out of her mouth, thin wisps of vapour rising from it.

"That's it, that's the one."

He's leaning back against the cold wall in the playground. He fumbles through his pockets, looking for a butt.

She swallows again and rises to stand beside him, tries to draw herself in close to him, seeking warmth.

"Watch yourself," he says, striking a match inches from the fringes of her hair.

She moves away from him, feels the cold suddenly, the sour taste at the back of her throat. She spits.

A minute later he's on his own. She's going all slippy-slidey again, careening across the pavement; losing sight of him further down the street.

"Wait a minute. Wait just a fuckin' minute!"

He lights yet another smoke. Tosses the extinguished match in the street. Rounds the corner, out of sight, all alone.

# A MONTH OF SUNDAYS

She likes the ritual: breakfast out every Sunday.

I've been meeting her at Dudley's Family Restaurant every Sunday for the past seven months. She always arrives before me. Tells me to meet her at nine sharp, but I normally straggle in around quarter-past. On the rare occasions when I have arrived at nine, or even five to, she's always here before me. She is—and always will be—punctual, proper, and predictable—like the sex we used to have, another Sunday morning ritual.

I brought coffee back to bed for the two of us. I sat and savoured mine. She propped herself up on three pillows, gulped her first cup and then read patiently for ten minutes, waiting for me to put down my cup. When I did, finally, she eased a hand over beneath the sheet to check if I was hard.

A minute later we were gnashing teeth and prying pyjamas from flesh, the caffeine kicking in. Once down to essentials, she played it cool, lay back, kicked out the blankets at her feet, and guided my head towards her centre, where I licked, her taste chasing the coffee taste from the floor of my mouth.

Half an hour later we'd be done. I became garrulous, yammering in the kitchen over a second cup of coffee. She became reticent, back to her book, on the toilet now, legs crossed, casually going about her business.

An hour later, showers administered, we'd go out for breakfast. But not to Dudley's. Another place. More upscale and self-important. Bailey's Bistro? I can't remember the name. Somebody's bistro. They've closed since.

Now it's only breakfast. She hasn't been able to drop this part of the ritual.

I sit, smile wanly, and a hovering waitress appears.

"Coffee?" she asks, although I have yet to refuse her these past seven months.

"Uh-huh," I reply, turning the cup over for her.

She fills it and drops cream and sugar.

I take it black.

Rosemary stares out onto the street.

We sit in silence for thirty, forty seconds, before the waitress returns.

"Ready to order?"

Unlike the bistro, they don't let you loiter at Dudley's. Breakfast is taken very seriously and served with efficiency.

"I'll have the usual," Rosemary says.

The waitress pencils it down on her pad.

"I'm fine with coffee for now," I say.

The waitress looks puzzled. She pauses.

"You should order something," Rosemary says. It's the first thing she's said since I sat down.

"You're losing weight. Eat something," she urges, like an insistent grandmother.

"Alright, okay," I relent, eager to be on solid ground with her, even if it's only over what I have for breakfast.

"I'll have the special," I say, unimaginatively. "Eggs, scrambled. Brown toast and, uh, bacon."

I turn to Rosemary. She looks satisfied.

The waitress scurries away, scribbling as she walks.

Despite the weather, we always walked breakfast off in the woods in Churchill Park, a block or two from the bistro. This meant traipsing through mud and clumps of rotting brown leaves in the rain in autumn, or sliding over slick, frozen trails in the winter. In fairer weather, we would settle into an unhurried gait, greet dog-walkers, dodge runners and mountain bikers, and admire the blooms around us. When we came to a clearing, we would stop, turn together and face the sun like a pair of heliotropic flowers, then drop to the earth and spread ourselves in the grass for ten minutes of ruminative sky-watching.

Today, mid-October, the midst of an Indian summer spell, would be ideal for a casual stroll through the park. But a walk together in the woods, like the sex that preceded breakfast, has been trimmed from the ritual as well.

We get caught up in the four or five minutes before breakfast arrives. There is very little that can possibly be new and exciting since we chatted seven days ago, but I run through the gauntlet of questions anyway.

"You keeping well?" I ask.

"Uh-huh," she replies, lifting her coffee cup and searching the bottom to confirm that it's empty.

"Job alright?"

Rosemary looks at me directly for the first time. She always does for this question. "Same shit. I'll get through it," she murmurs desperately.

"You looking for anything else?"

"Just thinking about looking, not actually looking," Rosemary replies. She puts her cup down and checks the street again.

"Heard from your mother?" I ask. Now it's my turn to reach for my coffee cup, something to occupy my hands.

"You know I have," she says sternly. "Dinner at her place every other Wednesday. Never fails. Won't take no for an answer. You remember how it was." Her voice trails off. I'm trying to figure out if she put emphasis on the word "was."

I slurp my coffee, which I know annoys her.

"Mom's getting old," Rosemary says earnestly, continuing. "It worries me sometimes. She doesn't cook like she used to. Much less variety."

I shrug, scalding my tongue with black coffee.

The breakfast arrives a minute later, a minute passed without further conversation. Platters of brown, yellow, and reddish-black food are placed strategically by the waitress in front of us.

"Enjoy yer breakfast," she quips and then darts away.

Food fills the aforementioned silence. We eat together solemnly, eyes coming up from plates occasionally, checking on each other, then skirting off to avoid contact, scanning the interior of Dudley's, or feigning interest in the pedestrians on King Street. A humble meal, the hub of our brief time together.


Fifteen minutes after they were dropped, the plates are taken up by the waitress. I wipe my mouth with a paper serviette and look at Rosemary. She is dressed in a billowy black sweater that shadows her lithe frame beneath. Her hair has grown long and is approaching the unmanageable phase. She wears neither make-up nor jewellery, and looks stoic in her mournful nudity. She turns and reaches for her wallet, distracting me from my inventory of her features.

"Thanks for breakfast," she says, although she always pays her half. She thanks me, more, for the company, strained as it may be.

Seven months, about thirty Sunday morning breakfasts together, and this is all she ever has to say. I've tried three or four times to bring up our past, to hint at some resolution, or at least lay my bargaining position on the table between us, but every time she deflects my words with an upheld palm, her face turned away, her mouth full of pancakes. I've always let it slide, knowing how she hates serious conversation over a meal.

Rosemary stands, pushes her chair back, steps to the side, and slides the empty seat back against the table.

"See you next week," she says, as I stare at the empty chair opposite me.

She won't leave until I grunt confirmation. When I do, I know exactly what she'll do next. She'll whisper a strained: "Good . . . See you then . . . Goodbye . . ." putting a hand on my shoulder as she passes. A dozen times, and again today, I've wanted to grab that hand and pull her face towards me until I can smell the coffee and syrup on her breath and kiss her sticky lips violently, tasting her sweet saliva on my scalded tongue. But I never do. I always let her go, let her walk casually out into the street.

Today—a warm Sunday in October—is no different. She pats my shoulder and glides out of the restaurant like a ghost. I look for her on King Street. I follow her image down the sidewalk until she is beyond my vantage, and then turn back to the empty table.

Another thirty seconds of silence, and the waitress arrives scooping up Rosemary's cash.

"More coffee?" she asks.

"Yes," I answer through a clenched jaw.

It's how I finish every meal. But still she insists on asking.

# THERAPY

"You should be thankful they're not staples."

"Staples?" Martin asks.

He's given a bird's-eye view of her yellow hair when she leans forward over him, shifting his smock to the left, exposing his groin. Martin's penis lies slack to the left, his testicles smeared against his inner thigh.

"Staples," she says. "They put staples in the head now instead of stitches."

Martin looks down at her from his pillow.

With fingers that are nicotine-stained and long she places a small stainless steel tray jotted with instruments next to his leg.

"I've heard that," he says. "But you can't be serious. Not there."

She laughs, selecting a scalpel and tweezers. She leans over him again.

"No, you're right; not for this."

Martin's nurse is in her mid-forties, her fingers bare of rings. He can't read the name on her I.D. badge wedged into her shallow cleavage. Her arms are razor-thin. Her narrow legs crossed on the edge of his bed. A white uniform drapes and dangles about her, as if she is a hanger in a closet. She has the body of a junkie.

She stretches the skin around his incision, pinning hair beneath her fingers. With her left hand she burrows into his testicles, pushing them to one side.

Martin makes some kind of noise.

"Wouldn't want that now," she jokes, the blade gleaming in her hand.

He grunts something back at her, his mind muddied with painkillers.

"This may pull a bit," the nurse says.

His genitals recoil.

With deft precision she removes each of his twelve stitches, discarding the thread on the tray. It does pull but Martin doesn't protest. His gaze is focused on her work.

When she finishes removing the stitches, the nurse leans in closer, inspecting her job. Her fingers glide effortlessly over Martin's new scar. The area is red and swollen. Pockmarks rise where the stitches once were.

"That doesn't look so bad," she says.

Martin is only four days out of surgery. He can feel her warm breath on his balls, just centimetres from her fingers. She hovers over him, engrossed in her work. The procedure complete, his cock stirs. The nurse bends back, selecting a tube from her tray and wipes Martin with an ointment, not warning him about the stinging, her eyes falling over him when he inhales sharply.

"You're all set then," she says a few seconds later, collecting her tray, standing beside him.

Martin lags his head left in his bed, eyes falling across her frail body beside him. Sunlight pierces her frame. He drops his gaze from her face to the gap illuminated between her thin legs. Her white uniform is translucent. She is not wearing a slip. Her legs are slightly parted. He can just make out the small mound at the crest of her legs. She holds the pose for a moment, aware he is transfixed on her, knowing his mind is messed with confounding sensations, before stepping towards him and smoothing his pale-blue smock with her free hand.

"Try to walk this afternoon," she encourages.

As she says this Martin is sure her hand deliberately brushes against his penis. It's not the drugs. He's sure she is checking for an erection.

"There's still some swelling," the nurse says.

He can't respond. He feels as if his arms are in shackles, as if his head weighs a tonne.

The nurse turns to leave.

"I'd like to see you pass by my station today. There's a cane if you need it."

She points to the door and to the corridor beyond, then leaves without a sound.

Martin turns away, peering out the window, into the sunlight, the city rumbling outside his hospital window.

◊ ◊ ◊

Jim visits Martin about half-past one. He is doing a two-week voluntary stint in the Psyche Ward three floors above. Every six months or so he has a breakdown of some sort on a Friday or Saturday night and winds up hospitalized. Before the Psychiatric Hospital on the mountain closed, Jim did several longer tours there. Once he was in the locked-end of a ward for three months. Martin visited Jim at that time, worried that Jim was on the road to permanent institutionalization. Hospital closures have since prevented that worry.

Martin and Jim have been friends for nearly twenty years, going back to grade nine when their lockers were side by side in the same gym class. They did drugs together in high school. Drank a lot. Went to parties together. Just the two of them showing up unannounced at someone's parents' house with a bag of grass and a bottle of rye, leering at girls clamped in the arm's of football players. After high school it was university. Neither Martin nor Jim finished. Three or four years they hung around the campus taking stray courses that didn't amount to anything. The drugs became harder.

Their time together diminished. Martin took to fucking women more. Jim took to bouts of reckless drinking that culminated in fits of depression. His hospital stays began about the same time.

In their final year at university, Martin had his first hernia operation, signalling the end of higher education for him. He had the surgery in mid-April, missing three exams. He could not be bothered to get medical slips verifying his ailment. He simply let school fade away in a Demerol haze.

Jim leans on the windowsill, obstructing Martin's view of the sun and sky. "The nurse said you should walk today."

Martin looks over at him. Jim appears angelic in the window, bright sunlight falling across his long brown hair. Martin murmurs an incoherent reply, his lips fat, moist, and numb.

"They're gonna want you out of here tomorrow. They don't let anyone recover any more. Nobody loiters here." Jim swings his left arm above his head, twirling it like a propeller.

Martin's eyes focus. Feeling slowly begins to return to his lips. He recalls where he is: in hospital, recuperating from surgery. He is speaking with Jim, an old friend who is essentially insane.

Jim continues. "Fucking government. They don't fucking care if anyone really is sick. They keep shuffling me in and out of here. In and out. In and out. None of it does any fucking good. They won't top up my disability. They say I'm not really sick any more. They talk about programmes and recovery and rehabilitation, occupational fucking therapy."

Jim's voice lingers, hovering in the thick, hospital air.

Martin shifts his attention to the scar on his groin. He slides his right hand under his smock, feeling the incision. A cool breeze glides across his skin. He thinks of the nurse and her cold steel blade. Her gaunt fingers digging into his testicles. The way she gripped his cock just before she left. He holds his erection in his palm. He tugs lightly at the head of his dick, the knuckles of his hand brushing against his new scar.

"Jesus, Martin! I'm talking here and you're playing with yourself!"

Martin hears Jim and turns his head. He looks over at his friend, appearing bewildered. He hears rustling and complaining from the bed to his right.

"What?"

He looks up at Jim.

Jim points down at his crotch. He apes jerking off.

"Fuck, knock it off."

"What?"

Jim rolls his eyes.

"You were playing with yourself. I could see your dick coming out of your gown."

"I was?"

"I wouldn't make that up, believe me."

It makes sense to Martin all of a sudden. He pulls his hand away from his groin and bridges himself up on his elbows. Thoughts of the emaciated nurse drift from his head. He focuses on Jim once more.

"Sorry, I . . ."

Jim waves it away.

"I've seen worse upstairs, believe me."

Martin opens his mouth but doesn't say anything. His erection dwindles. He looks into the eyes of his old friend, recognizing him fully for the first time this afternoon.

"Pull up a chair. Sit," Martin says.

Jim shuffles in slippered feet into the corner, pulling a grey chair to the edge of Martin's bed. He sits, staring at Martin, reaching out, holding his friend's hand.

"You should walk today. You don't want them wheeling you out in a chair tomorrow. Because they'll kick you out no matter what. It was just a hernia, ya know. Nothing that should really slow you down."

Martin stares at Jim, words spewing from his friend's mouth. He forgets for a minute that Jim is sicker than he is. Jim is the one who is infirm, who will likely never be well. In a few days Martin will be back at home taking steps two at a time, while Jim will be sliding drugs under his tongue.

"It feels better having the stitches out," Martin says.

Jim doesn't reply.

Martin sits up on the bed, ignoring the tug in his groin.

"Jim, did you know they put staples in people's heads now?"

The question lolls in the air between them.

"Jim?"

Martin puts his hand out, fanning it in front of Jim's face.

"Staples. In the head. Did you hear what I said?"

Jim smirks at Martin.

"That rhymes."

Martin laughs uneasily.

"I should go back upstairs. They'll be looking for me before too long. But before I leave, the reason I came down was to tell you that Maria is a patient here as well. She's a floor beneath you. I bumped into her at the canteen downstairs this morning."

Martin sits up further in bed, curious.

"She's getting her nose done later this afternoon. Can you believe it? After all these years."

Jim ambles away, towards the corridor.

"What room?" Martin asks, craning his neck.

"I don't remember. Or she didn't tell me. One floor down. Find out for yourself."

Jim steps into the corridor. His voice cackles back at Martin one more time.

"I told her you were here, that you'd drop in today."

Martin shifts his legs over to the side of the bed. Jim is well beyond earshot. He swings his feet one at a time down towards the floor.

"You cocksucker, Jim."

He looks out the window, sunlight glancing against his bare feet.

❖ ❖ ❖

When Martin passes by the nurse's station, the yellow-haired nurse who removed his stitches is not there. In her place an older, harsher brunette sits bundled in a cardigan sweater reading *The Weekly World News*. Martin leans on the ledge by the window.

"I'm up," he says.

The nurse lifts her heavy head from her paper.

"What was that?"

She has hands the size of steaks. Her arms are plump, sagging wherever muscle should be. Her uniform bulges at the seams. She has the body of a sumo wrestler.

"I'm walking," Martin tries again.

She looks back into her paper, oblivious to his accomplishment.

"Let me know when you run the marathon," she says. "I'll be there with bells on."

Martin finds it difficult not to laugh and tries to run a step to impress her. He feels his fresh scar cinch. He recoils, seizing his cane. His gaze drifts back to the fat nurse but he says nothing further. She ignores him, ruffling the pages of her newspaper.

✧ ✧ ✧

Martin steps out of the elevator onto the third floor. He reads red plastic signs lettered with white paint above him. He is dressed in a terry-cloth robe over top of his hospital smock. He drags his feet in slippers. His hair is greasy, piled on his head. Three days growth on his chin.

Leaning on his cane he shuffles down the corridor. Nurses whisk past, ignoring him. Doctors traipse by, their eyes centred on charts in their hands. A few stray visitors linger. Cleaning staff stare at mops that sweep across the linoleum, their eyes averted. A yellow tee-pee of a sign warns Martin of a slippery floor. He steps around the side of it and enters the first open room. It is marked with the name "M. De Silva." The second slot is blank.

Maria is in the bed by the window, resting before her surgery. Her window faces the same direction as Martin's, sunlight falling across the floor. A curtain partially shrouds her. Martin stumbles towards the bed. He can hear Maria's breathing, can smell her perfumed skin. He can imagine her black hair crested around her head, contrasting the dull hospital sheets. Rounding the edge of the curtain, he sees her fully. Maria is as beautiful as he remembers. His mind is clear and precise, the effects of the painkillers having faded. His scar throbs lightly beneath him. Martin is exhausted, but invigorated by his first post-operative jaunt—by the sight of Maria.

Maria isn't sleeping. Her eyes glisten with the glimmer of drugs. The sheets are pulled up to her throat. She recognizes him and smiles, mouthing the word "hello." Her lips are dry.

Martin doesn't say a thing. He leans the cane against the wall and stands to her left. He removes his terry-cloth robe, a sweat coming over him. Sunlight falls across his greasy hair, his unclean body.

Maria smiles still. Her left hand comes out from under the sheets, patting the mattress.

Martin doesn't sit. He stares at Maria's nose. It is prominent on her face, a beautiful central feature. A point of significance. He steps to her, reaching for her face. He slides a finger down the slope of her nose, caressing her smooth skin. At the tip he lets his fingers fall idly to her dry lips. Maria kisses him there, her tongue coming out, wetting her lips.

She sits up in bed. Still, Maria doesn't say a word. She loosens the sheets around her, pulling them back, revealing her blue smock to Martin.

Martin, his hand next to Maria's cheek, looks down at her body laid out on the institutional bed. Her breasts rise and fall beneath thin fabric. At her hips, the smock gathers slightly. Below her knees, Maria's legs are bare, her feet small. She has the body of a song: warm, familiar, inviting, something sweet on the tongue.

Maria reaches down to the hem of her gown. She tugs on it, shifting her weight. Her eyes are on Martin. He stares at the movement of her hands. Bundling fabric in her fingers, she hoists her smock up over her waist, exposing herself. Beneath the smock she wears white panties. At the hem at her crotch black hair tangles against skin. Martin steps closer. He stares at the hair. He follows it up the edges of her panties until it vanishes. He shifts his gaze across the top seam of her underwear. A small white bow is stitched into the centre. He looks at it for a moment, before dropping his gaze below to the mound of flesh that rises beneath the white cotton.

Maria reaches out with her left hand, taking Martin's right hand, trying to pull him towards her. Her eyes shimmer momentarily. She smiles and she says something, but Martin cannot hear her words. He loosens the strings on his smock, letting it fall to the hospital floor. He stands naked and skinny in front of her, then turns, offering Maria a glimpse of his new scar. She reaches for it, easing forward, her lips brushing against the new rise in his flesh, his penis mashed into her black hair. She draws her tongue across his severed flesh. Puts his cock in her mouth. Martin holds her head against him and slides his left hand up to her crotch. He places his hand on top of her cunt, feeling its warmth under his palm. He savours her lips on his flesh. He looks down at the tangle of black hair by his waist. He runs his right hand through Maria's hair, inspecting her scalp for staples. He feels nothing. Shifting his weight, catching his breath, coming, Martin falls into Maria. She looks up, eyes magnificent beneath him. Martin cannot say a word. The room is warm around them, almost humid. It doesn't seem to matter that they are trapped in a hospital. He holds his body against Maria, feeling his incision pulse. He looks into her face and lightly runs his lips across her nose. She kisses his cheek, her fingers caressing him. He has loved her always. She is graceful in his arms, from another time.

## SOME OF MY NEIGHBOURS

I'm watching a kid up the street kick a soccer ball off the front steps of his house. His mother sits on the top step and screams at him.

"Knock it off. Get in the house. You're gonna break something."

I'm at least one hundred metres away. I can hear her as if she is bellowing directly into my ear.

The kid ignores her. He keeps kicking the ball off the steps, laughing as he does so. Cars speed past on the street behind him.

"You gimme that ball. I'm sick of the noise," she screams, but doesn't budge from her perch on the top step. Then the kid kicks the ball too high and she grabs it. He squeals and she screams again.

"There. Now what are you gonna do? I've got your damned ball!"

His mother is wearing a pink sweatsuit and grey slippers. Her black hair is a tangled web of knots. She is overweight.

The kid is dancing a delirious jig around her. He wants his ball back. He is shrieking at his mother who ignores him.

Now he's really wound up. He's running up and kicking the bottom step and then running back to the sidewalk, wildly wailing the entire time. The scene embarrasses me. I want it to end. I want the mother to give the kid back his ball but she doesn't. She just sits there in pink clothing, the soccer ball nestled in the folds of fat on her stomach.

"GIMME THE BALL." Kick. Run.

"GIMME THE BALL." Kick. Run.

"GIMME IT NOW." Kick. And this time he runs too far and trips on the cement and falls into the gutter. A red car, with its stereo hammering, slams on its breaks and skids to a stop, its front bumper about a metre from the kid's head. The mother screams and bounds down the steps, scooping up the kid. She smacks him hard on the back of the head, then bawls at him, hauling him up the steps into the house where I can hear her slapping and smacking him despite his protests.

The red car pulls away slowly. The soccer ball has rolled into the street. I'm on my fire escape, watching.

# EXODUS 10

Darren's full of self-doubt, jealousy, rage, misdirected bitterness and a few other things. It spills over sometimes. Destructively. Stupidly.

"Karen. Karen, you fucking cunt! Get your ass back here!"

"Fuck off," she yells back.

He's standing in the corridor outside their apartment. Karen struts away. A fly buzzes past Darren's left ear. He fans air.

"Fuck sakes."

Mr. Ferguson in Number 8 opens his door as wide as the chain-lock will permit.

"Mind your own fucking business, ya old queer."

Ferguson's grey-haired, shrivelled head disappears. He goes back to watching television, darning his socks.

Darren ducks inside, scooping up Tiffany—their ten-month-old. He stands in the centre of their small apartment, holding his daughter, thinking. A few flies hover. Two fly in a triangle around the single bulb dangling from the ceiling in the living room. A steady, numbing rhythm. Darren watches the flies for a second then turns towards the door. He bolts out with Tiffany in his arms. Scrambles down the corridor.

Karen's halfway to the bus stop. He's in boxers, slippers, black, rock T. It's minus ten degrees. Pavement slicked with ice. Clear and cold. His breath clouds as he screams at Karen to wait. She says something back at him over her right shoulder. Tiffany—also underdressed—stares blankly, her small, frail body bobbing, jostling on Darren's shoulder.

Inside the bus shelter he pulls even with her. Karen's sucking on a butt. She's doing her best to ignore him now, anxious.

"Don't just fucking walk away from me. You know I hate that! Fuck sakes."

A woman in her forties feigns interest in an advertisement slicked behind glass in the shelter. A man in his fifties strolls outside to the sidewalk, head bowed; something fascinating him on the pavement. Tiffany droops her head onto her daddy's shoulder, blotting out the ruckus.

Karen rears her back to Darren, inhaling deeply on her cigarette. She eyes up the street for the bus.

Darren's getting really worked up now. He paces in the small enclosure, two steps one way, one and a half the other. Cramped quarters. The woman in her forties slips out to the street as well.

"You can't just fuck off to work again. I've had it with this."

He's pointing at something with his right hand, gesturing, left arm wrapped around his daughter.

"I spend all fucking day cleaning up Tiff's shitty diapers, feeding her formula, doing fucking laundry. I've had it. Not today."

Karen stubs her butt with her boot. She wheels to face him.

"It's what we got arranged just now."

"It's a shitty fucking arrangement, then," he spits back.

Tiffany mewls on his shoulder, shivers, snotty nose pressed into greasy hair.

"I can't wait for you to get off your ass and get a job. You can't fucking hold one. You get a job and I'll go back to minding the baby."

Karen gives him a crooked grin.

Here comes more of the vitriol spilling over, boiling over.

"Listen, you dumb cunt."

That word again.

"Listen to what I say. I say what's what around here, not fucking you!"

His face is the colour of a Valentine. Veins in his neck—bold, bright, distended. Right index finger rigid, jammed cock-like into her face.

"I'm not staying home doing fuck all all day. Looking after the baby while you're out working your shit job!"

Karen says nothing. She knows it makes him angrier. She lights up. Flicks a dead match on the concrete.

Another, on her way to work, arrives to wait for the bus. She, too, keeps a distance, minds the gap.

Tiffany doesn't make a sound. Not a peep.

Darren's coming unstuck. He's out of things to say for the moment. He seethes stupidly in one corner of the shelter. Sweats despite the cold. Beads of it on his nose, his upper lip.

❖ ❖ ❖

Karen works at the local Bi-Way stocking shelves. Cheap shit—household items, bathroom stuff, crappy kids' toys. She steals when she can. A bit here and there. A four-dollar doll for Tiffany. The head came off it last week. She makes eight something an hour. No benefits. Forty hours a week, sometimes more when she covers for one of the part-timers on Saturdays. She's been at it three months now. Her first job in four years. Back then it was a pizza parlour thing. All that time Darren always managed at something.

She doesn't like the Bi-Way job. Doesn't really dislike it either. Better than spending days with Darren. Nights are bad enough. Although he usually just pisses off to the bar when she gets home. Pushes the baby into her arms and vanishes. Or to his cousin Reggie's. They sit around watching truck-pulls on TV, drinking shit American beer. Or watching one of Reggie's pornos. He's got a collection. Darren comes home afterward buzzed on weak beer, forcing his fat dick into the small of Karen's back, groping her engorged breasts. She lets him have it once in a while. If the baby's not bothered. Or she doesn't. Mumbles "fuck off," and rolls away, tugging at the covers, desperate for sleep. He calls her a cunt and jerks off in the washroom. He's got magazines. Can't afford video tapes, never mind a VCR.

Darren worked most recently for Third Sector, sorting through recyclables in an old warehouse on Victoria Avenue North, the sort that typically go up in flames. That lasted ten months. Till four and a half months ago. Till not too long after the baby was on the scene. He worked separating plastics from aluminum from glass. Different types of paper once in a while. He hated it. Every minute of it. The only windfall was picking through discarded magazines. Those the guys on the trucks didn't pilfer. He found half a dozen skin mags that way. Old stuff; 1970s soft-lighted *Penthouse*. They were good enough for him. Chicks with weird, oblong breasts. Scraped the crap off the magazines and took them home. Stashed them behind the toilet. Karen reads them once in while on the shitter. Makes fun of him for it. When they were in better humour, she'd imitate him jerking off. Darren let her do it. Anything sexual. Sometimes she let him read the stories to her in bed; ridiculous tales. Let him fuck her, indulging whatever unoriginal fantasy came to his mind. But that was a rare occurrence. Now a distant memory. History.

◊ ◊ ◊

It comes to him suddenly.

"I spend more time with Tiff than you do and more fucking time with her than you do at work. It's not fucking right and I can't stand another fucking minute."

He shifts the baby from arm to arm. Tiffany sputters a bit and then sags in against him. Trying to keep warm.

Karen's getting restless. Her left leg twitches, a slight spasm. Darren's made fun of it before. Called her "gimpy." Right now there's nothing funny about it. She's aware of the stares of the others at the bus stop. People she sees every morning. Others on their way to work. She's said "hi" in the past; remarked on the weather. Had a brief conversation with the guy in his fifties. If Darren knew about that, there'd be fireworks.

She looks again for the bus, desperate for its arrival. Darren leans in closer. The gears in his head churning, burning oil.

"It's not fair and it's not right for a man. I feel like a fucking failure 'cause you gotta go out and earn a bit of dough. I still got Unemployment coming in. At least for another month. It's almost enough and then I'll go get a lousy job. Maybe me at the fuckin' Bi-Way. Keep you happy. Get you back with the baby where you belong."

He spins away from her again, speeding on adrenaline. Glares at the woman outside the shelter. She returns his look, condemning him with her eyes, pleading with him with her eyes to realize that he is making an ass of himself and of his wife in public. It doesn't work.

"You fuck off too, bitch."

He doesn't say it loudly, but loud enough.


Karen sees the bus approaching at last. She starts to step out of the corner of the shelter. Darren trots over, boxing her in.

"Where the fuck you think you're off to?"

Tiffany whimpers a little, sneezes, snot clogged in her nostrils now smearing her lips.

"I got work Darren. Lemme out."

She sounds desperate now, exhausted, exasperated. Her left leg throbs.

"Fuck you do."

He puts his left hand on her shoulder, wrapping his wiry fingers around her orange coat. It's padded for winter but she can feel the pressure of his digits.

"You're not going to work today. You're coming home with me."

She looks at him, the first hint of tears rising at the corners of her eyes.

The bus slows, breaks and idles at the curb. The other three duck up the steps, out of the cold, away from Darren and Karen.

Karen pulls away, ripping her arm from his grasp. But he reaches out and catches her again just so. Tiffany sneezes. More snot on her lips, drooling into her mouth.

"You come home with me, cunt."

As he says it he squeezes as hard as he possibly can, feeling his fingers boring into Karen's flaccid muscle, touching bone. She squeals. Looks him in the eye. The bus pulls away. He holds her in that spot, hurting her. Tears fall from her eyes. He gives one last hard push with his thumb and fingers, then lets her go. She collapses to the pavement, on her knees, and then is up again quickly.

"You fucker," is all she says.

Darren stands there, triumphant, lingering on the sidewalk.

Karen scrabbles away. She limps with her bum left leg. Breaks into a hectic, sloppy run, away from him, from her daughter. She can't catch the bus. She'll be late for work. She'll loose her job. Her arm aches. Tomorrow a purple bruise the size of a dollar coin will mark her. It'll change colour over the coming days: purple, blue, black.

◦ ◦ ◦

Back inside the apartment, Darren wipes snot from Tiffany's face on the hem of his black, rock T. He stares at the two flies still orbiting the light fixture.

"Fucking cunt," he says, referring to his wife, not to his daughter.

He parks Tiffany on the floor and gropes for the TV converter. She starts wailing. He ignores it. A fly lands on his
knee. He surfs then stops. On screen something eerie on the
Discovery Channel: grasshoppers up close. He shivers. The
fly leaves his knee.

Darren averts his eyes from the television to a window,
looking out on the grey, mid-winter street. There he sees a
cloudy formation, something blurred at its edges. It comes
closer. Right at him. He sits there, his heart hardened,
watching the apparition approaching. The sun is blotted out.
Black sky. A shadow falls across him. He can't see anything
but the dark mass. The sun and earth and moon cannot be
seen. Locusts. They fill the sky, the trees, the telephone
wires, the street, consuming everything in sight. Strange, in
mid-February. They knock away glass, pouring through
Darren's window, filling the apartment and all of the apart-
ments in the building and all of the buildings on the block.
He has never seen anything like this before. Not even on TV.
He thinks of Karen scurrying away from him. Wonders if the
locusts are after her as well, consuming her. Or if she is free,
let go.

The wind picks up, driving more locusts into Darren's living room. He just sits there, idle, letting them writhe and
crawl over him. Stunned into silence. Then he claws at his
eyes, trying to rid himself of the pests. He screams inward-
ly, his voice blotted out by the humming of locusts' wings. He
considers his actions from this morning. His wrong-doing.
His transgression. His hardened heart. But it doesn't move
him. Not a millimetre. He calls out again, shouting, shun-
ning the locusts. The insects retreat, the sun returning, the
light and the sky. The television burbles once more. He sits
and stews for a moment, his ears ringing.

A minute later, Darren jerks up on the couch. His head
aches. He eyeballs the TV. A Pharaoh's tomb being pillaged
on the Discovery Channel. He looks over at Tiffany. She is
silent, occupying herself. He looks at his arms; scratches at
bites and abrasions that aren't there. Brushes away unseen
locusts from his black, rock T. Goes for a piss.

Tiffany mucks in the corner. Her headless doll untouched. Cockroach turds all around her naked, blackened feet. A few mouse turds, too. She picks up one, rolling it between thumb and forefinger as if it were a Rice Crispie. She toes a littered beer cap on the scratched hardwood. Makes a clucking noise, typical of babies her age. Monosyllables. Her first word might be ball. Might be truck. Might be cunt.

# BUBBLE ROOM

I'm drawing a damp mop across the piss-yellow floor in Trevor's bedroom. Trevor is opposite me, sitting cross-legged on a chair in one corner of the room, watching me work. At this time of day patients are not permitted into their bedrooms. Trevor is supposed to be roaming the corridor, sitting in the TV room, or waiting in the waiting room for visitors who will never arrive. The poolroom is also an option. Bedrooms and the cafeteria are strictly off-limits.

In the morning, after emptying all the garbage cans on the ward, I dust mop and damp mop the washrooms and bedrooms. Afternoons, I dust mop and damp mop the corridor, from one end of the ward to the other, from the unlocked end to the locked end. Three times a week—but not today—I mop the cafeteria floor. Once a week I mop the floors of the TV room, the waiting room, and the poolroom, usually on Thursday. The decision is mine. Today is my slow day, the day that I clean only the washrooms, the bedrooms, and then the corridor. I am a custodian at the Hamilton Psychiatric

Hospital. I am responsible for the heavy cleaning on the D2 ward. I have worked here for eight months. I am paid $10.65 per hour.

For the past three months I've had my own ward. I work with an older woman named Agnes who is responsible for the light duties on D2. Each morning, when our shifts begin, we sit in virtual silence for half an hour—from seven o'clock until half-past seven—drinking instant coffee in the custodian's room. Agnes always arrives before me and puts on the kettle and the radio. She loves country music. At seven o'clock in the morning, tired and hung over, I'm not crazy about country. But I sit, drink my coffee, and let the songs wash over me. It's better than leaving the custodian's room to begin my work early.

Agnes has largely given up on trying to make small talk with me in the morning. We have exhausted most subjects. She still occasionally comments on some of the other house-keeping staff, trying to lure an utterance from me. For example, she will remark about this person or that person, or will talk about Ted who used to clean D2 with her. I've indulged Agnes once in a while. Told her that I have spoken with Ted in the parking lot. Told her that Ted is still driving his brown van. That he is not thrilled about being the custodian in the hospital's laundry facility; that he may transfer back to the wards, specifically, back to D2. But I make all of this up. I don't speak to Ted. I know what he looks like but that's all. I say these things to give Agnes the impression that she will have her old work-mate back, to reassure her, to put an end to our conversation. Ted likes to talk. Ted likes country music. Many times Agnes has told me this. Many times I have bobbed my head and slurped my coffee and suffered through her periodic verbal outbursts. But now, most of the time, the radio plays and we sit mute in the custodian's room, waiting to get on with the day.

I asked Trevor to move when I entered into his bedroom. I told him that he was supposed to be out in the corridor and that he would get in my way when I cleaned the room. Trevor hissed at me from his chair in the corner. I gave him a couple of minutes, but he didn't budge. I decided to mop around him. When I dust mopped, Trevor raised his legs in the air and laughed when the mop passed under his socked feet, claiming that I was tickling him. I looked into his dark eyes and didn't say a word to him. When I approached Trevor with the damp mop, he warned me not to get too close. He cringed, recoiling in his chair. I mopped quickly and then stepped away from him.

I'm now mopping around Trevor's bed.

"Don't get up to leave until the floor dries."

Trevor doesn't say anything. He stares at me, his eyes transfixed on my face. The only sound is the gentle swish of the damp mop fanning across the piss-yellow floor. I push a garbage can out of the way with my boot and mop the area of the floor where it rests. I then jam the mop against the edge of the bedside table and run it across the base of the wall, over to the door. I step up to the bucket in the doorway and push the mop into the filthy water. There are cigarette burns all across the floor, making it look spotted and bruised. I check my watch. I look at Trevor. He is scratching his goatee. He has eyes the colour of sewer water. His brown hair is thin, long and greasy, receding on his head. With a full beard, a crown of thorns, and a couple of Roman soldiers skewering him with spears, Trevor would look a lot like Jesus Christ.

"Serpents," Trevor spits.

I support my weight against the doorframe, blocking the way in and out of his bedroom. Behind me, patients and staff shuttle by in the hospital corridor.

"What was that?"

Trevor looks at me incredulously.

"Serpents. Coming out your ears. Big green ones. Crawling across the floor."

He points at the wet floor, his thin nicotine-stained finger trembling.

I look down, indulging Trevor's delusion.

"Not serpents," I say. "Just a mop."

I gesture to the mop and the bucket behind me.

Trevor doesn't look behind me and doesn't say anything further. He seems to be considering what I said about the mop, trying to decide whether what I have told him is valid or not. I stand and watch him without another word, waiting for the floor to dry.


I have four more bedrooms to clean and then that will be it for the morning, even though it is only ten o'clock. I'll spend the remainder of the morning playing pool, either by myself, or with patients. After lunch I'll quickly mop the corridor and then play pool until three o'clock, when it will be time to go home. The nurses hate it when I play pool with the patients. They have complained to my supervisor. When Mr. Watson, my supervisor, comes on the ward, I shrug my shoulders and tell him that the ward is clean, that all my designated duties are complete. To satisfy the nurses, Mr. Watson once had me clean the brownish-yellow smoke stains off the fluorescent light fixtures in the TV room with a rag and a bucket of soapy water while standing on a stepladder. But that's not my job, not part of my designated duties. I filed a grievance the next day and that was the end of that. Now I play pool in peace.

At lunch I will walk to Upper James Street and drink beer and eat fish and chips at Bernard's Tavern until ten past one and then come back to work half drunk. The nurses have also complained about my drinking, although only among themselves. I have heard them muttering when I push my damp mop down the corridor in the afternoon, swaying a little from side to side, once in a while whistling while I work. But there is nothing the nurses can do about my drinking. They can complain until they go blue in the face for all I care. From my point of view, D2 is my ward, my domain.

Trevor stands and walks across the wet floor of his bedroom, staring down at his feet. I want to holler at him; tell him that he is fucking up my clean floor. But I don't care that much. Instead, I step aside and let him slink out into the corridor. Trevor hisses again as he passes me, just centimetres away from my ear.

"Serpents," he whispers.

I look sideways at him. He has a look of absolute terror on his face, as if he is stepping into the express lanes of the 401 instead of into a hospital corridor. As he walks towards the TV room at the locked end of the ward, Trevor lifts his feet high up into the air, trying not to touch the floor. I think momentarily of Jesus walking on water and then scoff at the imagery, before turning away from Trevor and pushing my bucket to the next bedroom.

○ ○ ○

I once came across Trevor on a Friday on the Bruce Trail at the side of the Niagara Escarpment, outside the hospital. I was walking home from work. As it was Friday, I was fairly drunk. That day, after drinking at Bernard's, I brought a bottle into the custodian's room and drank vodka from my coffee cup and changed the station on the radio. Agnes came in at one point and said something about the noise. I may have been slouched on a chair, singing to myself. I cannot be sure.

At the time, Trevor was staying on the unlocked end of the ward. Counter to popular opinion, some patients are free to walk away any time they choose. The doors are open. The city awaits. And some do leave. One guy from B1 goes downtown once a week and parades around Jackson Square, gnawing on the palm of his hand and staring at his reflection in various mirrors. He is grubby and smells like hospital food. Mall security makes a phone call and the police bring him back to the HPH. One other time a woman got as far as Calgary. She was a patient on H2 and a nymphomaniac, according to Dave, that ward's custodian. I didn't ask

Dave how he knew this. I'm honestly not sure whether the nymphomaniac was brought back from Alberta. She's likely their problem now.

But Trevor isn't the type to wander away from the hospital. When I came across him on the Bruce Trail, he didn't recognize me, or pretended not to at first. Either way, he was confused. Then he began to quickly explain his predicament, saying that he had just walked out onto the back campus of the hospital to look out over the city below. He wanted to see if it still existed. He had no plans to walk down the escarpment but said that he had to piss, so he had entered the woods. I noticed that his pants were still undone and that his underwear was askew around his waist. Trevor gestured behind him.

"I pissed over there somewhere. On some leaves. They were dead. Then I ended up here. I don't want to go down but I can't go up. I think the leaves might kill me next."

Around Trevor, the leaves were turning and falling, the floor of the woods coloured orange, yellow, and red. I suddenly felt completely sober. Trevor looked like he was on the verge of tears. I walked over to him and pulled up his pants and told him to do them up. He couldn't smile at me or say anything further. He was still unsure who I was, but he did as I said. I walked Trevor back up the Bruce Trail and into the hospital. I led him back onto D2 without a word to anyone. When I turned and walked away, Trevor barked back after me. To the back of my head, he accused me of stealing his eyes, of storing them in a pickle jar under his bed. He said that he was going back to his bedroom to retrieve his eyes, to put them back on his face. He said he couldn't be fooled quite so easily. I let Trevor say these things without a rebuttal. Then I walked away, back down the trail, home for the weekend.

When I come back from lunch, Ted's talking with Agnes in the custodian's room. Country music is playing on the radio, the volume low.

Ted turns towards the door when he hears me come in. He's smiling a big idiot smile. A cigarette glows in his right hand.

"Better pack your bags, sonny boy. Come Monday, the ward's mine again."

I do not reply. I just jam my hands into my pockets and stand there, looking blithely at Ted, letting his words fall around me.

Ted is an enormous man. His head is the size of a rugby ball and is covered in thick, black, curly hair. He's missing several teeth. I notice this when he smiles. With him in the janitor's room, there is barely any space to move.

"What'd you mean?" is the best I finally come up with.

"I'm transferring back next week," Ted says. "Just here now to tell Agnes and to check things out on the ward. See how you been keeping it. The laundry is a fucking waste of time. You can have it."

He stops speaking to suck on his cigarette, then begins again.

"I got seniority. You can ask Watson 'bout it if you want. I'd talk to him if I was you, before he decides on his own where you'll end up. But that's your problem. Not mine."

Ted turns to Agnes and says something low—under his breath—which I don't catch. I can hardly see Agnes, Ted is so large. I can only hear her giggling at the other end of the small room. I look at the radio for a second, trying to discern the music. I think about the kettle and about making myself a cup of instant coffee. Not instant coffee; what I could really use is a drink, even though I just had four or five beers at Bernard's. Instead, I grab the handle of my mop from where it leans against the wall and wheel the bucket out the door. It's supposed to be my slow day. Regardless, I decide to wash the floors in the TV room, the waiting room, and the poolroom, just to get away from Ted. After that, I'll do the corridor. I walk away, leaving Agnes with the huge man in the custodian's room.

What Ted says may or may not be true. I'll find out on Monday morning. Watson may reassign me without a second thought. I've not been here long. Ted has worked at the HPH for ten years or more. I'm a junior man. I'll lose my ward if what he says is true.

In the TV room I mop the floor without first dust mopping. I simply sweep the cigarette butts and plastic coffee cups under the furniture with the damp mop. There are several patients in the room sitting in purple chairs, smoking cigarettes, staring blankly at the television. A soap opera is on. Bland, inoffensive, afternoon television. Trevor sits in one corner of the room, beside the TV. He isn't watching the soap opera. Instead, again, he watches me work. His eyes are wide and still look fraught with terror. I stop mopping and look at him. He opens his mouth to speak but doesn't say a word, and then doesn't shut his mouth. He sits there, slack-jawed, watching me watching him. A second later, Trevor stands and strolls across the clean, wet floor, his mouth propped open, his eyes centred on me the entire time as if tempting me to rebuke him. I say nothing and let him pass. I push the mop and bucket into a corner and then walk to the poolroom to play pool by myself. With the mood I am in now, the corridor can wait.

Twenty minutes later, Ted saunters into the poolroom. Without so much as a word to me, he grabs a cue and then the rack from under the table. He chalks up his cue.

"No sense playing with yourself," Ted says and then laughs, as if this is the most original joke in the universe.

I look over at Ted and nod in agreement, disregarding his remark. The cue in Ted's hands looks like a small, brittle matchstick. He racks and I break, scattering the balls across the green felt. The table's cover is faded, stained with food and spilled coffee and ripped in several spots. It doesn't always give a true roll. But it takes Ted only five or six minutes to defeat me. My mind is on other things and I don't play well. Ted slams the balls into the pockets viciously.

Four patients stand around, bored, watching Ted and me play pool. The patients don't speak. They stand in their socked feet, motionless. Their bath-robed bodies are oily and emit a peculiar odour, a consequence of their medication. They smoke cigarettes, drugged to the hilt, and gaze at the green table, mesmerized by the clashing and jostling of balls.

After the third game—all of which Ted has won—there is a commotion up the corridor. I hear nurses shouting and beckoning each other. One nurse, a small evil-looking woman in her forties, bursts into the poolroom. She glances at Ted and me playing pool and then quickly ushers the standing patients further down the corridor, towards the TV room. The patients move sluggishly away from us.

When the nurse reappears, she tells Ted to follow her. She looks at me, but doesn't say a word. I drop my cue on the table, following Ted and the nurse towards the commotion.

As we approach Trevor's bedroom, I realize that he is the centre of all the activity. One male nurse and two female nurses hold Trevor down on the floor, restraining him, just inside the doorway to his bedroom. Behind them, a female patient, an older, small woman sits on Trevor's bed. She looks terribly confused. Her blouse is torn at the shoulder and I can see the strap of her grey bra on her sallow skin. A female nurse has her arm around the woman's waist and is saying something in her ear. On the floor of the bedroom—the floor that I mopped a few hours ago—there is a small smear of blood not far from Trevor. Like the time I found Trevor on the side of the escarpment, his pants are open and his underwear is askew around his waist. I look down at him. He looks more terrified than I have ever seen him previously. The nurses are muttering in his ears, holding Trevor firmly, exposing their teeth like mad dogs as they speak to him. Below his opened trousers, there is semen on the leg of his pants.

Amidst the turmoil, I hear Ted say something to the nurse behind me. A second later, in one fell swoop, Ted steps forward and picks Trevor's crumpled body up off the floor. The nurses step aside, wanting nothing further to do with Trevor, and let Ted carry him like a baby up the hallway. Trevor doesn't protest. He puts one arm around Ted's neck and rests his chin on Ted's shoulder, peering back at us as he fades up the corridor. Tears streak Trevor's face. His hair is mussed. His goatee is caked in blood. I suddenly realize where Trevor is going: Ted is taking him to the bubble room.

There are no rubber rooms at the Hamilton Psychiatric Hospital. There may have been at one time but not since I've worked here. I do know, however, that electroshock therapy was a common practice at the HPH back in the sixties and the seventies. Shortly after I began working here, before I had my own ward, I once had to mop out a room filled with bizarre, medieval-looking apparatus, over by C2.

Each ward now has what is called a bubble room that is used for isolation, in place of a rubber room. The bubble room is barren, apart from a thin, grey mattress on the floor with no sheets or blankets and a bucket in the corner. On the door, a transparent, plexi-glass bubble protrudes into the room so that the occupant of the room can be observed without having to open the door. The nurse sticks his or her head into the bubble and can see every move the patient makes. Not that there is much activity in the bubble room. Most of the time the patient lies there, stultified and heavily drugged, until their incarceration lapses and they are free to wander the ward again. The room is seldom used and the patients hate it. Isolation is not the problem—that the patients are forbidden to smoke is what upsets them the most.

Ted walks back down the corridor without Trevor. I'm solemnly mopping the corridor, after having cleaned up Trevor's blood from his bedroom floor. The nurses have dispersed, back to their magazines, coffee, and smokes. The older patient has been taken away to find her a new blouse. I want to finish mopping the corridor and get the day over and done with.

Ted stops and stands beside me. He kicks the wheel of my bucket, trying to get my attention.

"You hear what Trevor was up to?"

I stop mopping and look at the big man.

"No."

"He was jerking off in his bedroom. Stuck his dick out into the corridor and grabbed Mrs. Savelli right when he came all over himself. Ripped her shirt. She socked him in the mouth and he fell down blubbering like a fucking baby. Miserable little pervert."

I look over at Ted. He lights a cigarette and stands there, waiting for me to say something, to agree with him about Trevor being a pervert. But I don't say a word. I just lean on my mop and stare down at the corridor floor. I hear Ted say something else but it doesn't register. I look up later and see him strolling away, down the yellow floor, into the custodian's room.


Five minutes later, when I'm almost finished the corridor, the evil-looking nurse approaches me. She doesn't know my name, even though I've been working on this ward for three months.

"Excuse me," she says.

I look at the nurse. Her face is scrunched up and wrinkled; a tight, ugly face with a small flapping hole for a mouth. I don't say a word and continue mopping the floor.

"Excuse me, sir," the nurse tries again.

I stop mopping and stare at her. I stick the mop in the bucket and stuff one hand in my pocket. I let her continue.

"Sir, Trevor's messed himself in the bubble room. I don't want that room to get all stunk up. Nurses aren't supposed to do any mopping. It's in the contract."

The nurse looks at me intently. I am focused on her tiny,

black hole of a mouth, words somehow escaping the cavity in her face. I want her to keep speaking. I want to see her small mouth open and shut. I want her to verbalize what she wants specifically. I will not interrupt, nor will I let on that I know what it is she expects from me.

"Your ward key opens the bubble room door," she says. "Could you do it now, before it starts to smell too bad?"

I hear the nurse's words but I don't acknowledge them. Instead, I want to ask her about Trevor. I want to ask her if it is true that he has pissed himself; and, if she really is concerned about the odour, then Trevor should be bathed, should be given fresh clothes, should be taken out of the bubble room. But I don't say these things. I'm only the ward's custodian, well, at least for the rest of the day. Nursing practices are not my domain. I have no say regarding Trevor's fate. Heavy cleaning duties are my territory. Nothing else.

I turn away from the nurse and her request and push the bucket and mop up the corridor to the bubble room. I stick my head into the bubble. Trevor is lying on his side on the mattress, facing the wall. The mattress is stained with piss. The floor is covered with piss. I can smell it from outside the room. I put my key into the keyhole and let myself in. Trevor doesn't budge. I don't say a word to him. I mop up Trevor's piss from the floor and then turn to leave, pulling the door closed behind me. It locks automatically. I don't look back through the bubble. I wheel my bucket and mop away without a word to anyone, back down the clean corridor.

## EUROPEAN WIFE

Kurt came into some money. The usual way when this sort of thing happens. A widowed aunt with a soft spot left him twenty grand. He got a letter from her lawyer. Really fancy stationery. Gold embossed lettering. Big fat cheque.

"Fuck me," Kurt said, turning the cheque over in his hand. He examined it from several angles. Held it up to a light bulb. Eventually convinced himself that it was the real deal. The teller at the bank didn't bat an eye when he slid it towards her.

"The works into my chequing account." He was proud and pumped. He wanted to ask the teller out but then got a glimpse of the rock on her finger.

A few days later he paid off his car. A few days after that he took Harry, Maria, Steve, and Anders from work out for supper and a good piss-up.

"It's on me," Kurt declared when the bill came.

"What the Christ?" Harry said. "You come into some money, big man?"

"Well . . . truth be told," Kurt said.

They all had another.

A week later he took a month off from the post office. He booked a flight to Rome. A Roman holiday. Twenty-eight days. The first time he'd been out of Ontario since he was a kid. Twelve years old back then, his dad packed Kurt, his two sisters, and mom into the car and they drove to Prince Edward Island. That was years before the bridge, of course. Took them three days. Stops in Cornwall and Edmunston. They drove straight through Quebec. Kurt's older sister, Sheila, had two years high school French. She interpreted road signs. "EST" was all the old man cared about. A week in PEI followed. Red soil. Lobster traps. Salt water. Anne of Green Gables. Japanese tourists by the busload. The works.

The drive back to Ontario's belly was even quicker: one night in a motel just *ouest* of Trois-Rivières. "Three Rivers" Kurt's dad insisted. Six months later the old man called it quits on a marriage of fifteen-plus years. Fucked off somewhere in Alberta. Kurt pictured cowboys and grizzlies and his dad in an oil field. No letters. No tears from his mother. A few cheques over the years without return addresses, most of them rubber.

From Rome Kurt took in some major stops: Florence, Genoa, and Venice. Kurt and a bunch of senior citizens in an air-conditioned bus. He didn't look at what the tour operator told him to look at. He drank wine at the back of the coach. Got a bit boisterous now and again. Puked once in the toilet in the back.

The final week he spent in Rome. He sat in cafés, crossed-legged, laughing to himself. He pretended he understood Italian, nodding his head as he eavesdropped on conversations. He whistled at women passing by. Drank very strong, very expensive coffee. Didn't sleep much. Started to grow a beard and let his face get good and tanned. Bought himself some gold jewellery from a vendor on the street. Haggled just a little.

Three days before he was due to fly back to Toronto he met Rena on the Via Crescenzio, not far from the Vatican. She was eating gelato. Had her sunglasses propped back on her head, keeping her hair out of her face. Kurt pointed at her shoes and made a face that said: "Beautiful shoes you've got there." Rena looked down, held her right leg out at an oblique angle and smiled. Half an hour later they were drinking wine and getting on in broken English. She was at least ten years younger than Kurt. Her father was dead. Her mother was veiled in black in a small town in the North. Sisters, brothers, dispersed here and there. One in Switzerland. She had cousins in Canada. "Winn-i-peg," she said. She knew it was cold, nothing more. Couldn't care less where the hell Winnipeg was. She laughed at Kurt's facial expressions. His splotchy beard. His slurred Italian phrases. Let him follow her home. Let him into her cluttered flat. Let him drink her wine. Let him spend the night. Let him do pretty much anything he wanted.

Three days later Rena was haggling with the ticket agent, booking a seat on Kurt's flight back to Toronto. Sometimes it really is this simple.

The karaoke night two weeks after the wedding was Harry's idea. But Rena caught the wrong bus and ended up at Limeridge Mall. Kurt waited for her for over an hour and then decided to panic. She made it home eventually. A bus driver named Frank—second generation Canadian—gave her the proper route number. Kurt called her at home. She answered on the first ring, on the verge of tears.

It was the shortest of honeymoons. Niagara Falls, of course. After all, it's so close. Rena couldn't believe it was just sixty kilometres away.

"Winn-i-peg. Nia-ga-ra Falls," she said. "I tod de water be froze all ah de time."

Kurt laughed and took her on the boat, the *Maid of the Mist*. Blue raincoats. Water vapour. Thundering falls. Later, dinner and a motel room. Heart-shaped bathtub. Great big bed. Satin, leopard-spotted sheets. Rena said it was "so stylish."

At the movies a week later Rena gave Kurt a hand job. They didn't sit in the back row. They were somewhere in the middle. The film was "so boring," Rena said. *Life is Beautiful*. It was the last thing Rena wanted to see. Kurt kept asking her if the subtitles were correct. Some people got up and left in a huff halfway through. Kurt untucked his shirt when the lights came on, covering the wet spot on his jeans.

Rena said: "Take me to Canadian movie next time."

Kurt laughed and thought long and hard about that. The last Canadian movie he'd seen was Cronenberg's *Crash*. He'd rented it for the soft-porn value and then recognized the highways in and around Toronto. "Next time, next time," he assured Rena and home they went, jiggedy jig.

The first time it snowed Rena burst into song: *White Christmas*. Christmas wasn't for another month or so. Kurt said, "maybe," then told her that the first snow never lasts.

Rena wanted to hear Bing Crosby.

"I've only got Sinatra and some Dean Martin," Kurt said.

Rena pouted. She wanted Christmas music.

Kurt told her Dean Martin was really named Dino Martini. "He was Italian," he said, trying to boost her spirits.

Rena looked up at him from the couch, arms folded in a funk across her chest. She couldn't care less if Dean Martin was from Mars. Didn't give a hoot for Sinatra.

The next morning she slipped on the walkway on her way to the grocer's. She sprained her wrist and bruised a knee. She learned to hate the snow along with everyone else. Like Kurt said, the snow didn't last. It rained Christmas day. It snowed between Christmas and New Year's. Then it went down to minus twenty-five and everything froze solid. Rena didn't want to leave the house. Kurt took time off from his postal route, the Christmas rush over. He finally persuaded Rena to leave the house. Drove her to Niagara Falls on New Year's day. He pointed out the ice. Rena couldn't believe the water was still falling.

"Never stops," Kurt said, teeth chattering.

They checked into the same motel, for old time's sake.

Rena told Kurt to invite the guys from work over one night to watch hockey. Maria came too. Kurt ordered pizza. By the end of the second period the Leafs were down and out and Harry was good and drunk. He wanted to dance with Rena. Anders protested. He said the Leafs still had a chance.

"They're down three goals," Harry said. "Let's put some music on and liven things up a little."

Anders watched the rest of the game with the volume turned down. Rena danced once with Harry—just the once—to get things going. Then she took Kurt's hand and led him round the room.

"Play me some Dino Martini, den," she called out.

"Wasn't Martini," Harry corrected from the couch, beer bottle wedged in his groin. "It was Crocetti."

Rena glared at him. "I like it better Martini, like de drink."

Harry shrugged and took a hit from his beer.

Kurt put on *Relax-ay-voo*. Old Dino sang along with Line Renaud. Rena squeezed Kurt with all her might. Bit him right on the ear, right there in front of everyone. Maria smiled. Harry fell asleep on the couch. Anders watched the Leafs lose 6-2 to the Phoenix Coyotes, the team formerly known as the Winnipeg Jets.

In the summer Rena started a garden. Tomatoes, peppers, green onions. She made fresh salads all summer long.

Sitting in the shade of an apple tree, Kurt watched Rena at work in the garden. She was bent over crops. She was sweating. She was whistling *White Christmas*. She was wearing the flimsiest of summer frocks. Sweat visible on the backs of her brown thighs. An apple fell from the tree to Kurt's left. He remembered his mother, suddenly. He'd have to call her one day soon and invite her round for supper, introduce her properly to Rena. Kurt's mom had been in hospital at the time of the wedding. She wasn't fit for a shock of any sort. She still didn't know Kurt and Rena were married. Kurt's mom was divorced now more than twenty-five years.

From the garden Rena called to Kurt. She yanked a carrot out of the ground and held it up.

"Beautifool carrots," she said and smiled.

Another apple fell from the tree. Kurt looked up at the branches above him. The sun pummelled his face. Blinded for only a second, he tried to find Rena's image again. He could hear her voice. He could imagine her yellow frock. Her eyes. Her tanned legs. The precise point where her legs became ass. He blinked twice, three times. His vision cleared, eyes watering a little. And then there she was, like she'd been standing there all his life.

# NOSTALGIA

Friday night the telephone rings at about 9:30. I'm unwinding over cold pizza and cold beer, watching Friday Night Football on TSN. I'm mildly interested in the Blue Bombers versus the Alouettes.

Three rings and I answer.

"Richard?"

"Uh-huh."

"It's Laura."

I pause. Think, Laura who?

Her voice registers: Laura from the realm of the recently divorced. Laura from university days. Days long since passed. Ten years ago we drank hard together but we never slept together. It's a lingering regret that still crops up when I bump into her.

I last saw Laura about six months ago in Limeridge Mall. I was lost in the consumer muddle, searching for The Bombay Company. She appeared by my side magically and directed me to the store. She was stunning, of course. She had a certain radiance in the dim, shopping complex light. We made small talk and got caught up. Laura was then about two months from the beginning of a ruthless divorce. I learned about her marriage collapsing several months later from a mutual friend over drinks in Hess Village. I barely batted an eye when I heard the news. At the time my attention was riveted on a middle-aged woman slumped at the bar on my left.

"You busy tomorrow, Richard?"

I don't answer immediately. I'm still hungup on a missed sexual escapade from some time back in 1987.

"Richard? You there?"

I grunt, confirming my existence.

"Because if you're not too busy tomorrow, I've got a proposition for you . . ."

I mute the television. Tracey Ham scrambles silently on the artificial turf in Montreal. I caress the bottle of Red Baron in my right hand.

"I've got nothing planned," I respond, oblivious to the consequences.

"Then I have a favour to ask . . ."

I have passed the point of no return. Whatever Laura asks now I am obliged to indulge her. It's my reward for not listening, for being more concerned with a meaningless mid-season football game.


I, too, was married once. Straight out of university I married another girl I drank with. She came to McMaster from Chatsworth, a small village split in half by Highway 6, about twenty kilometres south of Owen Sound. She made the two-hour trip to take Phys-Ed. Then, it was supposed to be a teaching degree, followed by a hasty retreat back to small-town Ontario to live out a life of normalcy. But the proverbial cart was overturned after only six months. She got swept up into the thick of things and was lost in the undertow. Her Phys-Ed degree changed to French, then to Women's Studies, and finally to the cozy confines of Sociology where she eked out the minimum requirements for a three-year degree. Teaching plans were abandoned. So was the retreat to Chatsworth. She decided to stick it out in the city, an outcome I had something to do with.

We ran in the same circles, drank in the same bars, puked in the same bushes, once in a while fucked in the same bed. We settled into this familiar pattern until I was poised to graduate and she was still jumping from one programme to another. Threatened with abandonment, she latched on to me like a lamprey.

We were married six months after I graduated in a chapel just outside Chatsworth on a road that meanders to Meaford. We divorced fourteen months later in a lawyer's office in Hamilton on Main Street East, five lanes of one-way traffic cruising by outside the window.

The Blue Bombers are kicking off to the Alouettes. Ham's scrambling led to an interception that was promptly converted into six points. Trevor Westwood, looking impish behind the single bar below his chin, sends the ball sailing back to Montreal.

Laura's voice cuts through my reverie. "Because I've been invited to Charlene's wedding tomorrow and I don't really want to go alone . . . I know it will be awkward for you . . . but I could use the company . . . use a friend."

I should be listening to Laura's words. Specifically, her continued reliance on the word "use" but I am still paying more attention to the game. The Alouettes bring the ball back to their own thirty-seven. Ham trots out onto the turf, a new series of plays churning in his head.

Charlene's wedding? It hits me suddenly. I don't want to think about how unwelcome my face will be at that event, or how uncomfortable I'll be when I knock shoulders with Charlene's dad—my ex-father-in-law—at the bar. As in the past, he will have no more than half a dozen words for me.

"Sure." It comes out somewhat slurred, even though I'm only on my second Red Baron. I may be anticipating the twelve or fourteen drinks I will have tomorrow at Charlene's father's expense.

My only wish is that the reception is not in the same dreary community centre where Charlene and I celebrated our nuptials: a trite, barn-like structure that possessed all the elements of scary, small-town Ontario. A Union Jack and a portrait of some long-since-dead local Orangeman hung on the wall. Dinner was served by a slew of featureless faces, who, along with the kitchen staff, shared no more than three surnames among them.

"The wedding's in Toronto," Laura says, disrupting my flashback, washing away the hick-town clichés.

But at the same time the Alouettes are pressing and I feel a sudden need to absorb myself in the game. I feel some affinity with Ham and his plight. I want him to answer with six points of his own.

"I'll swing by, pick you up at noon," Laura suggests. "You're being a good friend, Richard."

I mumble something back at her, again oblivious to Laura's coded language. I should be registering the word "friend." But I don't.

Laura thanks me and I fumble the phone towards its cradle.

I wonder for a second how she knows where I live.

Then it's back to the game. Converter in hand, I unmute the television. The Alouettes have come up short. Their few loyal fans scream for them to go for it on third and two. Ham looks over to the coach for guidance and then to the scoreboard, checking the time remaining. The first half is winding down. This is the right time for some CFL-styled drama. But there is sufficient time for gambling later—the coach concludes—shuttling the field-goal unit out onto the field. The crowd boos. I finish my beer. Ham looks expressionless, resigned to his duty.

❂  ❂  ❂

Charlene is wearing a cryptic-looking, nicotine-yellow dress. It's all sashes and sequins. My first thought is that I don't know how she got into it but I have no worries about being the one to get her out of it. That honour today belongs to another.

The ceremony is high Anglican in downtown Toronto. The weather co-operates. It's a beautiful September afternoon.

From my vantage point at the rear of the church I examine the backs of heads in front of me. I recognize farmer's haircuts and slightly shrunken suits. The women are adorned in colourful hats and all manner of dresses spanning broad backs and shoulders. From back here I can't see my former in-laws. They are surely crowded into the front pew, their thick palms splashed with sweat, their brows dewy and moist, praying—no, yearning—that Charlene is second-time-lucky.

At the reception at a swish country club within city limits, I feel sorry for Laura. She should have declined the wedding invitation and spent another Saturday night with another Harrison Ford movie. She looks slightly sick and it's not the wine. Amazingly, with more self-control than I could ever muster, she has limited herself to two glasses and will be able to drive us back to Hamilton.

But the entire thing is obviously too much for her on the heels of her messy divorce. Drink firmly in hand, I wonder for a second why divorces are always described as "messy." It sounds as if blood and other bodily fluids are spilled: a perfect image to clog my head at my ex-wife's wedding.

All my efforts to cheer Laura are lost in the tide of saxophone from the band. She doesn't want to drink. She has refused my invitations to dance. She appears committed to gazing blankly around the room, her head crowded with images of revellers celebrating a new union. I realize soon enough the futility of my quest to distract her and decide to concentrate on getting good and drunk instead.

The showdown with Charlene's dad never transpires despite countless trips to the bar. On manoeuvre number eleven or

twelve—when I have long since given up on politely asking
Laura if she would favour a cocktail—I meet up instead with
Charlene and question mark directly. I didn't read the
inscription on Laura's invitation, or listen to the vows, so I
honestly have no idea what his name is.

"Richard, this is Charles."

There's my answer: Charles. How regal and distin-
guished it sounds. Charlene and Charles. They even look
alike, the narcissism running amuck.

I'm not sure if Charles realizes that I am the Richard, but
he greets me gracefully and loiters for a moment before
striding off, leaving me alone with my ex-wife for the first
time in ages.

We have very little to say to each other, which is just as
well. I refrain from complimenting Charlene on her dress,
choosing instead to flatter her hair, something I recall she
always appreciated. I am, despite my drunkenness, miracu-
lously non-confrontational. I am not at all bitter or envious.
I offer no sarcastic remarks. No coy slugs at Charles rise in
my gullet. I behave completely out of fashion. For some inex-
plicable reason I am simply not an asshole at all. This con-
fuses me and I stumble for words.

But as quickly as she appeared, Charlene vanishes back
into the crowd—a smoky, yellow apparition, off to sow more
small talk.

"There goes my ex-wife."

I actually stutter this ridiculous phrase to myself and
hear it come back at me. Thankfully, glancing around, there
is no one within earshot.

With my drink in hand, I realize that we are finally finished. I no longer hold a place in Charlene's life. She is moving on. It is over. A few muttered phrases and promises
endorsed by the church have trumped the court's authority.
She is with another, now.

My head bobs and sways as I sputter incoherent nostalgia to
Laura on the QEW. She is sober at the wheel, sombre still.

She is uninterested in my epiphany, my realization that
Charlene has moved on with her life. I try not to sound too
liberated or sanctimonious, recalling Laura's pain, her
recent divorce. But then again I never liked Laura's knob-
head husband. He's a lawyer from Ottawa—which should
say it all—who condescended to socialize with Charlene and
me half a dozen times. After that he was forever "on business," an excuse that didn't sit well with me. The feebleness
of the excuse bothered me more than anything else. This,
and Laura's predicament. It was clear back then that she
had no future with the prick. Years later, Laura is crammed
into a compact car, using all her resolve to stop from begging
me for silence.


On the curb outside my apartment—of all places—I slide my
hand down the back of Laura's dress and dig lightly into her
ass with my drunken digits. Her left hand is braced defen-
sively on my clavicle. She will endure a few moments of my
come-on, giving me the opportunity to recognize my vulgari-
ty, and then gently push down on my collar bone, easing me
away.
    This is exactly how it happens.
    I kiss Laura's cold throat three or four times, feeling
absolutely nothing from her. I try to ease her ass into my
groin, gauging only resistance. Stupidly, I persevere, rubbing the small of her back with my palm. This is it. Laura's
hand on my shoulder shifts and she inhales deeply. She is
on the verge of explanation but I save myself the humiliation. I back off, defeated on my home turf.
    But what the hell do I want from this, anyway? A mercy
fuck for me? A comfort fuck for Laura? Do I really think this
is even a remote possibility? How is it that I behave like a
perfect gentleman with Charlene and Charles and then a
lecherous prick with Laura? I have only added to her grief.
    But then again, why is Laura so untouchable? She has
always been this way. We have danced this dance before,
years ago, mind you, back in university when we were both

pissed, but even then she shrugged me off. There was always something condescending about it. Something that said I never had a chance. That she was then—and would be forever—completely unattainable as far as I was concerned.

All of this flashes through my mind at the moment of rejection. Laura's behaviour bothers me more now than it did years ago. Back then her attitude was too easy to dismiss. Then, I really felt nothing for her. I was just trying to get laid. But tonight I want her in a different way. I may be pissed but I actually believe I want to comfort her, that I am capable of such an act.

Instead, I get a patronizing kiss on the cheek as Laura turns away from me. A few seconds later I am offered a mere glimpse of Laura's sacred, unapproachable body as she slumps into her car: a sliver of leg displayed amidst the folds of her black dress. Ten seconds later she is pulling away from the curb without so much as a wave.

Inside my apartment the answering machine offers no wisdom or succour. My stomach lurches: booze sloppily mixed with a plate-full of midnight sweets. I spy yesterday's pizza box at the summit of a heap of garbage in my kitchen. In my best black suit, my tie still snug against my neck, I gather the refuse and trudge towards the cans in the alley at the side of the building. I deposit the waste and then cast a sceptical glance towards the city's star-less firmament. There is no comfort there, either.

On the verge of stupid despondence, I start shuffling back to my flat, my bladder bloated. I am drunk again. I am alone again. But I refrain from muttering any more clichés about women; circumspect that I might embarrass myself before the racoons pawing split bags of garbage, rummaging through my leftovers.

# LET ME TELL A LOVE STORY

Kevin rides the bus with Helen every week day morning. She lives two doors down from him on the first floor of a red brick house. Helen has lived in the neighbourhood for twenty-five years. Her family once occupied all three floors of the house at Number 36 Sydney Street. She has raised three children, all of whom have moved away to other parts of the country.

Helen was married to Ernest. He left her three weeks after their youngest child Ilsa migrated west to Calgary. Ernest retreated alone to Belgium, the country in which he was born, the country where all his memories were housed.

When Ernest left, Helen took a job dispensing coffee, doughnuts, and muffins in a small chain-shop in the Eaton Centre. She has been working there six years, taking only two weeks off each summer to fly to Vancouver where her children congregate for a family reunion. Marc and Mara live in Vancouver. Ilsa comes west from Calgary. Apart from this summer ritual, Helen doesn't see her children. Marc, Mara, and Ilsa have families of their own, children who are largely unfamiliar with their grandmother. Christmases for

Helen are spent alone on the first floor of the former family home. She receives a telephone call from each of her children Christmas morning, wishing her well. The grandchildren are usually too excited to wish their grandmother back east "Merry Christmas." They run past the phone, dodging the out-stretched receiver, busy chasing childhood distractions.

Helen is a speculative woman. She has shared with Kevin her opinions on many subjects during Sunday mornings when he walks past her house. She has invited Kevin to sit with her on the stoop of her veranda where she has eyed the headlines of the newspaper in his hand, commenting on the situation in Quebec, or youth crime, or the unemployment rate.

"The Quebecois don't know true suffering," Helen has said, prior to vocalizing her position fully. Or, "Children from shattered homes never know true love and strike out at all they see." Or, "There are jobs for everyone, but too many people don't want to work at jobs they think are beneath them."

Helen feels strongly about the last subject. She has told Kevin about the tired souls who wander up to her coffee counter complaining about jobs that don't pay well, that are completely without interest. She has no sympathy for young men in suits and trench coats waiting for their idea of a perfect job in a bank; balding, fattening men who turn away all opportunities presented to them.

Kevin listens to Helen's observations. She never rants. She speaks with the wisdom of her age. She is a grandmother. She has raised three children. She lived with a man who didn't love her and left her alone. She is nearly twice Kevin's age—about sixty—yet she has the vitality and vigour of a much younger woman. Helen has wit and a certain lingering beauty.

She isn't bitter about Ernest leaving her. She speaks openly about him with Kevin when the subject is raised, when Ernest slips into the conversation. There is no nostalgia wavering in Helen's voice. Ernest—Helen has told Kevin—was a man mad with memories of the past. He despised every minute of the twenty-five years he spent in Canada, toiling in the heat and the din in one of the city's enormous steel plants. He made a respectable wage. He was aware of his responsibilities. Ernest cared for his children, spending his money to meet their needs, to ensure that they were well clothed, fed, and cared for. He wanted Marc, Mara, and Ilsa to be educated, free to choose an occupation better than his. He wanted his children to be strong, independent. When he was convinced that this had happened, he believed he was free to leave.

Ernest spent none of his wages on Helen. He resented her tearing his memories from him, for up-rooting him to run off to a strange, cold country on the other side of the globe. It was Helen's idea to emigrate to Canada. "For the children. For their future," she had said a thousand times to Ernest. Helen believed the opportunities abroad were abundant, that her children would prosper in a new country, away from the incestuous shortcomings of their small hometown.

Ernest only allotted Helen small sums of money from his wages to be spent on the needs of his children. For her first twenty-five years in Canada, Helen wore only clothes brought with her from Belgium: dresses frayed and foreign-looking; sweaters darned at the elbows; under-garments grey with age, perforated with holes.

It took Ernest only a few weeks in Canada to realize that he no longer loved his wife. The woman he married in Belgium he left behind—another memory. Marc and Mara were born in Belgium.

In the new country Ernest tortured Helen with his misery. Weekends he would lie on top of her in their cold bed, pinning Helen's arms to the mattress, forcing himself into her, all the while muttering contemptuous phrases in her ear while he fucked her, devoid of emotion. Ilsa was conceived this way.

Ernest began squirrelling his money away and strategizing his departure. When he fled six years ago he left Helen

with a paltry sum of money and the house in her name. He
vanished without a word one morning on his way to Stelco.
He drove out onto the highway, east through the maze of
ramps and lanes to Pearson International Airport, and
boarded a flight to Amsterdam. From the Netherlands, he
took a train to Belgium, back to the town he had left a quarter century earlier. Old friends welcomed him back, men
shrunken and grizzled, none of them bothering to ask about
Helen or the children.

Saturdays in fair weather during the spring, summer and
autumn, Helen stands with a garden hose in her hand on the
concrete walkway that leads to her red brick house. For
hours she sprays cold water at the pavement, scrubbing the
stones clean of dirt and filth, ferrying unwanted debris out
into the gutter.

On the bus Helen sits with her purse nestled above her
knees, her hands folded in her lap. She is a tidy woman. The
uniform she wears at the coffee shop is always trim and
clean. In warmer months she sits only in her bright yellow
blouse, offsetting her brown trousers. She wears sensible
shoes: soft runners with comfortable soles that do not aggra-
vate her while standing over her pots of coffee. Her hair is
long and yellow still, which is unusual for an older woman.
On workdays it is done up in a bun and secured by barrettes.
There is only the slightest tinge of grey at the brows and by
her ears.

    Helen's face doesn't reveal her past. Her skin does not sag
with age. Her eyes are not murky with fatigue. Looking upon
her, one would not guess that she has endured a loveless
marriage; that she lives alone and unwanted in a large
house; that she works for minimum wage in a coffee shop in
a dismal shopping complex.

    Most mornings Helen manages a smile for Kevin at the
bus stop. She arrives before him and keeps her eyes fixed up

the street, searching for the bus. On board she may offer a few kind words.

"Nice morning this morning, Kevin. Everything fine at work? Stop in for a coffee if you have the time. Nice to see a young man so sure of himself."

Kevin responds to her remarks with courtesy.

"Thank you, Mrs. Dysma. It is a fine morning. Warming up nicely. I will stop for coffee if I can. Very busy in the office this time of year."

They exchange little more than polite remarks on the bus. Helen smiles at Kevin and then turns her head to watch the buildings pass by: more red brick houses plotted with gardens and lawns, laced with decorative trimmings, awnings and fences; so much pride on display on the small rectangles of property. Shops sail past as well: antique stores, pawnshops, second hand bookstores, all cluttered with unclaimed detritus. Helen and Kevin pass schoolyards chock full of shrieking children, children saddled with the simplest of responsibilities: arrive at school on time, find your way home, stay clear of trouble. Doctors' offices, bureaucratic complexes, hotels, and theatres loom as the bus approaches the centre of town. These buildings stand above Helen and Kevin, the lower floors shields of glass that throw shimmering images back at the bus—rippled passengers' faces that seem to dance in false light.

But Helen knows nothing of dancing. She sits stoically in her seat on the bus waiting for her day at the coffee shop to begin. She is sombre and quiet, her fingers occasionally shifting on the straps of her purse, her wedding ring tarnished with the years. The day holds little charm for her.

Helen rises before Kevin and walks to the centre doors to de-bus. She nods at him on the street, a half-smile forced on her lips and then merges with the crowd of pedestrians.

Some days Kevin will see her again. When he can spare the time, or when his mind drifts back to Helen and her drab polyester uniform, he will skulk out of his office, walk the three blocks to the Eaton Centre and queue in line for coffee at her booth. It amazes Kevin to watch Helen work. She is diligent and meticulous, serving her customers with efficiency. When he stands before her, Helen greets Kevin.

"Nice to see you, Kevin. You haven't been by in a while. Can I get you the usual?"

The usual. The phrase warms him before the coffee arrives. Kevin slips the necessary coins into Helen's palm, thanks her, and then retreats back to his office. This small moment goes further towards boosting his spirits than Helen will ever know.

Saturday mornings there is no bus to catch. Kevin walks past Helen's house on the way to buy a newspaper. He gives Helen a half-wave. In warmer months Helen is immersed in her sidewalk-purging ritual, her head slightly bowed. She gestures towards him. Kevin mouths the words "good morning," rounding his lips in an exaggerated fashion. Helen always nods her head and eases the pressure on the nozzle, making sure that Kevin's feet are not splashed. He passes by unharmed, and carries on his way.

Sundays require another newspaper. On Sundays in good weather Helen will sit on her veranda gazing down on her pristine, concrete walkway and beyond to the sidewalk.

These are the days Helen stops Kevin for conversation when he returns with his newspaper. These are the occasions when she has told him her views on religion, politics, societal woes, and her past. Her voice is always weak at first from lack of use, then stronger, her accent as pronounced now as it was in 1976 when she arrived with Ernest and their two small children.


One Sunday Helen stops Kevin with a polite cough. He waves towards her and says, "Good morning."

"Lovely morning," Helen corrects, her voice strong.

Shielding his eyes with his fingers, Kevin looks up at her.

Helen is sitting in an old, wooden rocking chair, her legs crossed. She is wearing a sun hat, although she is shaded on her porch. Her yellow hair drapes down casually onto the shoulders of her white blouse. She is wearing a light blue skirt that comes down just over her knees. She is smartly dressed in clothes purchased with wages earned at the coffee shop. But she is also bare-foot, her left foot on the floor of the veranda, pushing off slightly, her body listing with the action. Helen looks content and happy in the new day. It brings a smile to Kevin's face.

"Come talk to me, Kevin"

Kevin stops at the end of her walk.

"I'm off to get my paper. When I come back?"

He says it without realizing the ignorance of his rejection. But Helen smiles on. Kevin has never seen her in a mood like this before.

"That can wait. There are newspapers each and every day of the week. The news comes and goes but a day like this is a rare thing."

Kevin finds it difficult to disagree. Also, he is intrigued by Helen's philosophical demeanour. She is beaming from her rocking chair. He stands at the end of the walk, looking up at her. Helen stops rocking for a second and shuffles her chair forward, the sun splashing across her bare feet.

"Besides, Kevin dear, I made fresh bread this morning."

The phrase echoes in his ears. Helen has never called Kevin "dear" before. It mesmerizes him for a second. But the phrase also reminds Kevin of Helen's age. She is a neighbour who has lived here almost as long as Kevin has been alive. She is from another time when simple phrases like "dear" were bandied about to comfort visitors, friends, and family alike. Kevin looks up at her from the pavement, locked in indecision.

"Come, Kevin, before it gets cold."

Helen stands quickly and beckons him towards her door. The chair rocks lightly without her. Kevin steps up the clean walkway and follows Helen through the front door into her kitchen. The aroma of fresh bread works at his senses. The bread scent is mingled with the scent of the house: a mixture of perfumes, soaps, carpet deodorizers, and Helen herself.

He has never actually been inside Helen's home before. The interior of the house holds sparse décor. In the kitchen,

postcards from British Columbia and Alberta and photographs of blonde children of various ages are taped to the
fridge. A solitary table with two chairs sits against the wall.
On it, a loaf of brown bread simmers. By the back door that
leads to Helen's yard, a large suitcase—packed and labelled
with an address tag—awaits.

◦ ◦ ◦

Mrs. Crompton in Number 39 has told Kevin a lot about
Helen. Mrs. Crompton has lived on Sydney Street since 1965
and is now a widow. Her husband died six years ago, only
weeks before Ernest left Helen.

Kevin shovels Mrs. Crompton's snow each winter, clearing the walkway so the mail will get through. Mrs. Crompton
has few visitors but is obsessed with the arrival of the mail,
wishing daily for a letter from her sister in England or from
one of her three daughters dispersed across Canada.

Kevin intervened to help Mrs. Crompton with her snow
six years ago. Mr. Crompton died in February—the month
when a disproportionate number of older people die and
when many others opt for suicide. That February Mrs.
Crompton was knee-deep in a leap-year blizzard, her frail
body twisting in the wind, snow whirling about her. When
Kevin trudged across the street and offered his services, he
heard her curse two things: the wretched Canadian winter
and her recently-dead husband.

Over cider, Mrs. Crompton shares her version of neighbourhood history with Kevin, recounting families long since
moved away: the Underwoods, the Millers, the Kaleskis, the
De Marcos, the Shavers. Upon hearing these family names,
Kevin imagines an era captured by black and white photography, characterized by large cars with rotund bumpers
and children playing innocent, now-obsolete games in the
street. Sydney Street in Kevin's imagination is a pristine
strip of virtuous families who know nothing of separation,
deceit, or infidelity. Like the cider, the vision warms him.

The warmth is lifted when Mrs. Crompton speaks about

Helen. She has told the story of Helen and Ernest to Kevin several times. She has told him about Marc, Mara, and Ilsa: three children who seemed too eager to leave the family home, obsessed with careers, unconcerned with their mother. Ernest left, according to Mrs. Crompton, on a warm, early-spring day: the frost was just coming out of the ground, Ilsa was not yet a month in Calgary, and Ernest was deserting his car at the airport, boarding a plane with one suitcase of belongings. He was a sour man. His contempt for Helen was made clear over the years. The woman that Ernest despised and abandoned is the same woman that Kevin knows, the woman with soft, yellow hair and a smile each morning on the bus who toils at an unrewarding job, grasping longingly to a life that seems to lack reason.

◦ ◦ ◦

Kevin's house is also red brick but only two storeys. He moved into it five years ago when he finalized his divorce. Kevin's wife kept the house in Kingston, while he moved south-west to Hamilton to take a job in a city where he knew no one. It was the sort of clean break he needed.

Kevin's ex-wife—also named Helen—fucked other men, all professors at Queen's University.

While Kevin worked as a computer programmer, Helen took a second degree. She said she was interested in history and that she needed a second teachable subject. Kevin indulged her, supporting Helen while she sorted out her career options, wading slowly through the academic mire, trying to find a way to make use of an Arts education. Kevin went straight through university into a decent job. His skills were easily applied. Helen was another story, a story that became all the more lucid and lurid as the courses at Queen's dragged on towards nothing.

Helen fucked professors, often in their offices, the curtains drawn when office hours ended. Young professors and old professors. Professors from Europe with bad wardrobes and body odour. Professors up from the States with boundless arrogance. Dour, Canadian professors who whimpered when they lay on top of her, their semen smeared on her thighs.

The professors signified something pristine to Helen; that was all the explanation she offered when she sat down with Kevin five years ago and confessed her infidelity. She wanted to muddy that pristine image.

Kevin listened as these words fell from Helen's mouth, his hands clenched in his lap, fingernails biting into his palms. He stood when Helen finished speaking and struck her once across the face with an open hand, his skin wet with perspiration. The slap was quick and made a sharp sound. The legal proceedings that followed were to the letter, all wrapped up in a tidy package.

Kevin's mind, however, was not so easily cleansed. The weight of Helen's deceit followed him when he quit his job and retreated temporarily to his parents' house in Ottawa. He maundered for two months before taking a new job in Hamilton. He drank and didn't shave. He went days without bathing. He trawled through the market leering drunkenly at prostitutes, muttering to himself under his breath. Despite his lust and his internal rage, Kevin lacked the resolve to approach the women working on the street. Other women in bars, cafés, shops, at the train station or bus terminal were also unapproachable. Kevin could do nothing apart from stare, his lips unmoving, his legs cemented in his stance, his head clouded with indecision. Eventually, he left his childhood home bitter and confused and moved into a simple house on Sydney Street in a city he knew nothing about.

◊ ◊ ◊

Helen urges Kevin to sit at her kitchen table. She sees him eyeing the suitcase by the back door. Kevin's mouth falls open but he says nothing.

"The bread must have cooled by now," Helen says, cutting through the silence.

Kevin leans towards the loaf and inhales the fresh scent. It smells like heaven.

"I only have tea. I can't stand the smell of coffee in the house."

Kevin looks over at Helen. She is busy at the counter across the kitchen from him. Her back is turned. She is searching her cupboards for mugs. She is up on her toes, her bare feet tensed, the calf muscles in her legs flexed. Her blue skirt slides from side to side, gently brushing the crooks at the backs of her knees.

"Tea is fine," he says, his mouth parched.

Helen serves him bread and blackberry tea. The kitchen fills with the aroma of the two. She sits across from Kevin at the small table, her elbows propped, her hands wrapped around her mug of tea. A smile shapes Helen's face.

They make conversation. Helen seems obsessed with the weather. She can't stop exclaiming about the beauty of the sun this morning. Behind her, the sun rounds towards the afternoon, beams of light splashing down through the back door onto the suitcase, a dim shadow creeping across the floor.

"Are you going somewhere?" Kevin says, pointing towards the case.

Helen continues to smile. She places her mug of tea in front of her and centres her eyes upon him.

"I had a telephone call last night. Ernest is dead. I'm flying to Belgium this evening to see him put into the ground." Kevin shifts the empty mug before him on the table. The loaf of bread is nearly half-finished. Crumbs are scattered between them. He wants to offer sympathy, the expected reaction. But Helen's expression and mood denies any need for sympathy. She is nearly happy, surely pleased with the news.

"Who called?" is the best he comes up with.

Helen waves away the inquiry.

"Kevin, enough. What does it matter? We should enjoy the morning."

He wants to correct Helen. He wants to tell her that the

morning has almost passed, that the sun is high in the sky. But there is no logic to offering this observation. Kevin sits instead and relishes Helen's happiness. She is clearly not interested in discussing Ernest's death. He has never seen her so content.

When it is obvious that Kevin has nothing further to add to Helen's pronouncement, she stands and clears his mug and plate away. She leans in towards him, that smile still etched on her lips. Prior to walking to the back door, she turns lightly on her bare feet and places the dishes on the counter.

Helen stands over the suitcase, revelling in the warmth of the sun. Her arms are folded across her chest. Her back is to Kevin again. She rocks lightly on the balls of her feet.

"Come look at the view," Helen says, without turning to Kevin.

He stands and walks to the door. His left foot brushes against the suitcase. Helen points to a tree in her backyard filled with birds. Kevin leans to look through the window, his head just left of Helen's shoulder. She speaks to him and turns her head. Her eyes alight and she shifts her torso towards him. Helen says something more about the birds. Kevin stubs his foot on the suitcase. He is not looking at the birds. He is looking into Helen's eyes. Her eyes are deep blue and moist, tears welling in the corners. She says something further about the sun. He leans closer, as if he cannot discern her accent. Tears overflow onto her cheeks and run across her smooth skin. He has nothing to say to comfort her. He leans closer still, inhaling Helen's scent. His cheek brushes her hair. He puts his right arm around her, holding Helen. She leans her body weight into him. She is warm under his touch. Her head comes up to meet him. Her tears are centimetres from his lips. Kevin wraps his left arm around her stomach and then slides his hand under her blouse. He rides his hand up to her breast, cupping its weight in his palm. Helen's breast is warm, heavy. He squeezes it slightly, fingering the nipple. She doesn't say a word as he leans and licks the tears streaking her cheeks.

Helen smiles and her lips come towards him. He parts his lips—wet with her tears—easing his weight into her, kissing Helen under the glare of the afternoon sun. Her mouth is warm, moist, comforting. Kissing Helen is just as Kevin has imagined a hundred mornings on the bus.

# THE JOB

My first day on the job was six years ago. "The job." That's what the white hats called it. To the rest of us it was simply known as garbage.

I put in for the transfer and it came through eight months later. I wanted out of the Districts. Too much bullshit work: cutting grass, pulling sewers, patching roads, shovelling snow, picking trash downtown when they had nothing else for you to do. You never knew what it was going to be from one day to the next. Plus, the dog-fucking and hiding from the bosses started to get to me. It made the days long. I just wanted to do the job, then go home. That's why I put in for garbage. You did your work; you fucked-off home. Simple as that. Or so I thought.

I walked into the garbage yard the first day at quarter to seven. Kerwin, the foreman, gave me shit straight away. He said he had me assigned to Marshall's truck and that they always leave the yard by six-thirty. How was I supposed to know? Two minutes on the job and already I was getting grief. "You're stuck running with Tindale's gang, then," Kerwin said.

He was holding a stubby golf pencil and a tiny black note-book. His dyed hair was slicked back. His trousers pressed. He wore cowboy boots that were definitely not City issue. A gaudy silver watch jangled on his wrist.

"Who's Tindale?"

Kerwin didn't look up. He continued scrawling in his lit-tle book.

"Truck 49. That's where you'll be stuck till I tell you dif-ferent."

I found the empty, idling truck and climbed into the cab. It stunk but I was expecting that. The seats were torn and frayed. The driver's side was swaddled with one of those beaded covers. At my feet, muddied skin mags were strewn about the cab's floor. I looked around the yard. Groups of men of all ages in green pants and bright orange T-shirts huddled in various camps: smoking, drinking coffee, spit-ting, some of their lips moving. I saw Kerwin and a couple of other bosses hovering, darting from camp to camp like hummingbirds, issuing orders, their heads bowed over their books, pencils scratching in knobbly hands.

I checked my watch. Five to seven. I reached to the floor and pulled out a soiled copy of *Swank*. I flipped through pages cluttered with vile images of woman probing their dis-tended crotches, fingering fat and fake breasts, lips puck-ered, eyes gazing forward, looking completely deprived of emotion. I heard the cab door open.

"You'll go blind looking at that shit."

I turned right, facing the source of the voice.

"Kerwin said we had a new man. Push over. Make room."

I did as instructed.

"I'm Tommy," he said, not offering a gloved hand.

"Matt," was all I said.

"Yeah. Kerwin said as much."

Tommy was facing forward, staring through the truck's windshield. He must have been in his early fifties. It was impossible not to notice the boils marking his face, neck, and forearms. A tattered ball cap perched atop his greasy hair. His City issue jacket was faded and worn. And on a Monday morning, when most people were either still sleeping or slurping coffee over their waffles, Tommy Tindale stank of booze. It wafted from him like some kind of rancid cologne.

"So, what kinda name's Firth?" he asked, eyes still forward.

"Sorry?"

"Firth. Where're your people from? And I don't mean what part of the city."

I shuffled in my seat a little.

"It's a Scottish name, I guess. Maybe English."

Tommy turned to face me. His eyes were bugged out. Saliva glistened on his lips.

"You mean you ain't sure where your people come from?" he said, as if I had just confessed to the most heinous of crimes.

The strength of Tommy's denouncement, plus the stench of his breath, held me speechless for a minute. I was about to try redeeming myself when he leaned across me and blared the horn. I shrivelled back away from him, afraid the boils on his arm would somehow rub off on me. Tommy slouched back into his original position next to the door, his right arm folded out the window.

He muttered, "Well at least you ain't Portuguese. Had one of those pork-choppers from the Districts on the job last week. Dumb fuck didn't have a clue."

I dropped the *Swank* on the floor, not replying to Tommy's spiel. He mumbled something further but I missed it. A few seconds later the driver climbed in: a short, fat guy choking on a cigar. He didn't say a word. Just popped the truck into gear and we were off.

I was the proverbial rookie on the job back then. Even though I was at least twenty-five years younger than Tommy, he ran me into the ground. He slurred orders at me for the first hour, gave me a quick demo on how to charge the hopper and told me to watch out for cars. That was the extent of my training. Not that you needed much for grunt work.

I spent my first two months on garbage with Tindale. After sixty days, the roles had reversed. He was dragging his ass trying to keep up with me. I never harassed him about it. Tommy was, after all, old enough to be my father and a veteran of almost three decades of throwing garbage. But I pushed too much, just by working the job too hard. Kerwin stopped me one morning on my way to the truck and told me to run with Stevenson's crew. I guess Tommy had approached him and asked for a slower, older man, someone he could keep up with, someone who wouldn't disrupt his routine.

Six years later I had had my absolute, fucking fill of garbage. I don't know how Tommy lasted as long as he did. My fingers were gnarled and the nails had all fallen out after grabbing thousands of bags and cans. My back ached constantly. My knees popped and cracked when I walked. My feet were a mess. As was my head. I knew why Tommy stunk like a distillery on that Monday morning six years back. I, too, developed a bit of a problem in that area. But, if there is one cardinal rule about garbagemen, it's that they drink. Before the job. On the job. After the job. Always. And wouldn't you? Six, seven hours a day up to your chin in everybody else's filth and rubbish. And you wouldn't believe the weird shit I've seen put out in the garbage: bloodied sheets, a bucket full of dentures, boxes stuffed with the most horrid pornographic magazines (donkeys—there were actual shots of donkeys in some of them), bushel baskets jammed with hundreds of pairs of soiled panties (someone's private collection found and tossed out, in all likelihood), and unbagged dead dogs and cats, rigid paws pointed heavenward like unearthly handles, the bodies teeming with thousands of maggots. Do you have any idea how foul the stench from a colony of maggots is at eight in the morning when you're not sure whether you're hungover or still half cut from the night before? Not pleasant, believe me. And the bosses, speaking of maggots. Christ. The bosses were constantly on your ass, pushing, never believing you when you told them the truck was full, sending you out for a third run on a Friday afternoon in the middle of an August heat wave. Complete pricks, the lot of them. And I told them so enough times. It earned me three suspensions. I grieved each one but even the union couldn't save my ass.

Six years after I started, I put in for a transfer out of what I'd thought was the best job in the City. There was simply no such thing. Until my transfer came through, the bosses threw me back on the slowest truck in the yard, back to where I'd started, back with old Tommy Tindale, who was still drunk as ever, still foul-mouthed and covered with six years worth of new boils.

Tommy was still running with the same driver. Pete somebody. He was fatter, balder, and didn't remember me. Tommy grunted when he saw me back on his truck. He knew the score, knew why I had been reassigned to his run.

"Just don't kill the job," he mumbled. "I only got two weeks left of this shit."

I had no idea Tommy was retiring. I felt somewhat nostalgic when he told me, honoured that his last days would be with me. It was a small thought, the type you come up with to help pass the time.

On Tommy's last day, a bunch of the guys were milling about the yard, waiting to say their goodbyes. Most had worked with him at some time over the years.

At ten to seven when Tommy finally walked in from his bus ride, there was mild applause, hoots, and back slaps. Tommy waved it all away. I was standing by the truck watching him. At this distance I sensed his embarrassment. He didn't want the attention. It looked more like he wanted to get through the day and put the job to rest. Kerwin, still looking more like a pimp than a foreman, was all smiles, like he had some part in all of this, like he was the reason Tommy survived thirty-three years of throwing garbage. He shook Tommy's hand and flashed a smile. Tommy shrugged, rearranging the battered gym bag on his shoulder. And that was pretty much the end of the roasting. No speeches. No toasts. No gold watch. Tommy just shuffled away from a few stray jeers and headed to the truck.

I was still standing outside the cab. As he drew closer, I opened my mouth to speak. Tommy cut me off abruptly.

"Save it. Don't need to hear fuck all from you . . . Let's just finish the fucking job."

He was not what I would call gracious. But I knew what Tommy meant. The job had pretty much ruined his life and saved it. It had been a curse and his only blessing. I understood why he wasn't feeling overly sentimental.

Without a word, I followed Tommy into the cab. Pete sidled up and slid his fat ass behind the wheel. He was smiling. He reached under the seat and hauled out an unopened bottle of rye. Tommy's eyes lit up for the first time that morning.

"Now there's a man after my heart," he said, reaching for the whisky. He had the bottle open before Pete could get the truck into gear. As we pulled out of the yard, Tommy took a hit from the bottle and held it aloft out the window towards Kerwin. The bosses looked up at us as we passed. Kerwin's face was dour, completely blank. Tommy didn't say a word.

"Fuck 'em all," Pete said, as we hit the street.

I sat between them, not offering my opinion.


I watched him closely on his last day, but Tommy didn't waver from his routine. He worked as hard and steadily as he always had. He staggered a bit more than usual, feeding on the bottle of rye the entire morning. He muttered to himself but that wasn't unusual. He looked over at me once in a while. Gestured with his ragged, gloved hands at piles of garbage. He said typical things about how heavy the garbage was lying for a Friday, about how a third run was likely.

When we stopped after the first run for breakfast, Tommy came into Rankin's Restaurant with us but didn't eat anything. He never ate on the job, regardless of how long the day was. He smiled at the waitress. Took off his ball cap.

Used the washroom. And then placed his mysterious phone call from the pay phone in the corner. As Pete and I stuffed bacon and eggs and toast into our mouths, Tommy yammered away on the phone across the way. I recall him doing this every morning, never knowing who he was talking to.

Through the second run Tommy didn't falter. He shared the bottle a bit more. We had it polished off completely by eleven o'clock. Pete smiled behind the wheel. I shuffled along, slowed by the big breakfast and the equivalent of six or seven shots of rye. Tommy, who had had at least twice that, blundered on.

We finished our second load and had it dumped by quarter to one. Eight and a half tonnes. A respectable load of garbage.

As we pulled out of the incinerator and started heading back to the yard, Kerwin intercepted us. Pete tried to ignore him but there was no way out of a predictably terse conversation. Kerwin pulled his pick-up along side us. He jumped out and climbed up to the driver's side of the truck.

"How much?" Kerwin asked, his head halfway inside the cab, sniffing for something—not booze, that was a given. Fear, maybe, the dog that he was.

"Eight and a half," Pete grunted, the smile gone from his face.

Kerwin murmured something and then looked over at Tommy and me. I returned his glare. Tommy faced forward, unable or unwilling to look Kerwin in the eye one last time. The empty rye bottle lay on the floor atop the usual matting of skin mags.

I waited for Kerwin's decision. I was sure he was going to put Tommy through one last hour of agony before cutting him loose. If Tommy would only look at him, I thought, there would be no way Kerwin would send us back out for another run. Tommy would just have to ask—to flash that sly, drunken grin of his and Kerwin would surely take the high road. But Tommy didn't move. He just stared forward like he had done a thousand times before, waiting for his fate to be doled out.

"Call it a day, then," Kerwin said suddenly. "Looks like your men have had enough, Pete."

That was it.

Pete said something back at Kerwin, but Kerwin was already climbing into his pick-up, racing off to fuck-up somebody else's weekend. Tommy still didn't speak. Pete then slipped the truck into gear and pulled away from the curb quickly, fearful that Kerwin might change his mind.

On the way back to the yard Tommy said something to Pete that I couldn't make out. A couple of minutes later Pete stopped the truck outside the Carlton Tavern on Barton Street, a few blocks from the yard. Tommy grabbed his gym bag and slid out of the cab. I waited for him to make some kind of remark, to give some indication about the meaning of the day. I wanted him to offer some words of wisdom to us. Or make a joke about not seeing us Monday morning. But he said none of these things. Tommy just shuffled away from the truck towards the bar, like he had done most days. He half-turned after three or four uneven paces and waved back at us. His face was blank. His boils were prominent in the afternoon sun. He still had on his filthy gloves. And then he was gone, into the Carlton, to spend the rest of the day drinking.

That was it. Another man just walked away from another shitty job. There was really nothing to celebrate. The job had worked Tommy into the ground. Nobody would miss him. Things would carry on as usual. Garbage would pile up. Bosses would give orders. Come Monday, as the cliché goes, it would be the same shit, different day. A modern truism, if there ever was one.

# KISSING THE CABBIE

For the third time in the past eighteen months, Frank Morton has lost his job. Two days ago he was let go. Fired. Frank had been working in an office; some sort of government office, doing some kind of menial, ambiguous job that offered no future, no security, no gratification, no reward. He was hired on a short-term contract that was due to expire in three months. He lasted six of nine months.

Frank is riding in the back seat of a cab. He snaps his fingers quietly to himself and stares at the back of the driver's head.

"Just a few more blocks, then let me out at the light."

The driver bobs his head without saying a word. He drums one hand lightly on the steering wheel, keeping the beat to the song on the radio: an old Kinks tune from the sixties about a man dressed like a woman.

Frank leans forward, placing his hands on the lip of the front seat. He turns his head and speaks directly into the driver's right ear.

"You mind this type of work?"

The driver twitches away from Frank, as if a mosquito is buzzing in his ear, offering no reply. He glides the car towards the curb and turns down The Kinks. He puts the car in park, punches the meter, and slouches in his beaded seat, his shoulders shrivelling down towards his elbows pinched in at his sides.

"Six fifty-five."

The driver's eyes are set off to the left—away from Frank—watching two women loitering on the street corner, each with a paper cup of coffee in hand, each with a kinder-garten-aged child leashed by their knees. His head lolls slightly towards the women outside the window. His grey eyes glaze over. He yawns, his left hand coming up to cup his gaping mouth.

In the back seat Frank fumbles in his pockets, withdrawing a handful of change. He counts seven loonies and stuffs the remaining coins back into his trousers. He leans towards the front seat again.

"You didn't answer my question," Frank says, scattering coins on the seat beside the driver, edging in towards his ear. Frank's lips are no more than six or eight centimetres from the side of the driver's unshaven face.

The driver peers peripherally at the money beside him. He nods his head again while remaining mute. The fare has been paid. He is waiting for Frank to leave the cab. He does not want to answer Frank's query, to engage Frank in con-versation of any sort. With his right hand the driver gathers the money and watches the rear-view, waiting for Frank to leave. He starts to rifle his pockets for change, offering a sig-nal to Frank. Wordlessly, Frank slides across the seat, steps out of the cab, slams the door, and marches across the street towards a bus shelter. As the cab pulls away, Frank turns, spinning on his heels, and blows a kiss back at the blue and white car, a dim smile riding across his colourless face.

In the bus shelter Frank takes a seat on the metal bench. He gazes at the advertisements plastered inside the glass that frames the structure. A map of the city coloured with lines indicating bus routes fills the upper half of the shelter's wall on Frank's left.

He stands and observes the lines deviating off in different directions, cutting the city into various geometric shapes, bisecting neighbourhoods, indicating points of importance, beckoning visitation throughout the urban mass. With his right index finger Frank follows Route Seven from his current location, down to the city centre and back. He grins and fumbles for change, reading the list of fares written in bold, black ink in the bottom left corner of the map: Adults: $1.85. Students/Seniors: $1.10. Children: 75¢.

Frank holds a two dollar coin in his hand, turns away from the map, squats and bowls the coin on its gilted edge across the shelter's paved floor. The coin makes a slight scraping noise and veers left, out the shelter's door, across the sidewalk, plunking into the gutter. Frank, his face pressed against glass, rises up on his toes and watches the coin—his fare—glimmer in the street, the morning sun catching it just so.

A man with a briefcase in his right hand enters the bus shelter about quarter-past eight. He carries an umbrella in his left hand. He peers at Frank planted on the metal bench and then turns away abruptly, his left hand coming up, his coat sleeve coming down, the umbrella flashing in the air, all in one fluid movement. He checks the time. He looks up the street. He takes a half step towards the shelter's door.

"Late for work?" Frank says, his hands rooted in his pockets, plying the coins and keys that mingle there.

The man does not respond. He completes his full step with another half step and now stands half in, half out of the shelter.

Frank tries again, feigning a posh English accent. "Excuse me, my good man. Marvellous morning for a bus ride. I

asked you whether you are late for work. Did you hear me?
Are you late for work? Are you late for work?"

The man with the briefcase and the umbrella eyes Frank
directly. He squares his shoulders, clamps his jaw as if he is
suffering from a terrible toothache and mutters through his
grimace, "No, I am not late for work."

"I am!" Franks fires back, his voice rising to an absurd
crescendo, the fake English accent gone.

The man steps quickly away from Frank, repositioning
himself outside the shelter, concealing himself behind the
advertisements.

"Coffee with your tea? Coffee with your tea?" Franks mutters, giving up on his first visitor, snapping his fingers to an
unheard rhythm quietly to himself.


Twenty minutes later, two boys, aged thirteen or fourteen,
enter the shelter, knapsacks draped over their shoulders.
They are dressed the same: the Euro-soccer look, shimmering blue pants that fall lazily to their running-shoed feet,
team sweaters with logos splashed across red material. They
ignore Frank and banter back and forth to each other. They
are discussing teachers at their school: which ones are assholes and which ones are cool. The list is stacked in favour
of the assholes. They pay no attention to Frank.

Frank stands and stretches, farting. He smiles at the
boys and laughs to himself. They abandon their discussion
for a minute and stare at Frank.

"You say something, Mister?" one of them asks, laughing
to himself, nudging his friend to be sure he got the joke. The
other shimmering youth clasps a grubby hand over his small
mouth and bellows with laughter.

Frank, his hands out to both sides, his fingers pressed
against the shelter's glass, steps towards the two boys.

"My name's Frank. Frank Morton. Just to be sure you
know I'm not a stranger. You know what they say about
strangers, eh? Do they still warn you kids about talking to
strangers? They should. But I'm no stranger. Oh no. Not at

all. Must be clear about this. To clear the air and all that," Frank says, completing his diatribe, fanning his left hand behind him, waving away the odour.

The two boys, wary, but amused, laugh uncomfortably. One of them opens his mouth and begins to speak. Frank throws a hand into the air violently.

"Teachers and their dirty looks. Teachers and their dirty looks," he chants, staring down at the two boys jammed at the opposite end of the shelter. "Come on, join in. You know it." He waves his hands in the small enclosure, his fingers sailing through the air, flashing by the boys' faces. "You know the words. Don't leave me here making a fool of myself."

Frank begins to flap his arms wildly in the air as if he is drunk, hyped-up, conducting a bizarre orchestra. "Teachers and their dirty looks. Teachers and their dirty looks. TEACHERS AND THEIR DIRTY FUCKING LOOKS!"

The two boys, terrified, slam into each other in their desperate attempt to leave the shelter. They race down the street away from Frank, their knapsacks bouncing off their narrow backs, their outfits glistening in the morning sun.

Frank grunts and inspects the palms of his hands for some clue, before repositioning himself on the metal bench.

Ten-thirty, after a brief nap, Frank sits up. An old woman trundles into the shelter, a nylon bag bulging with produce by her feet. She keeps her eyes forward, avoiding Frank's intrusive gaze. He takes an inventory of her features: turquoise jacket sagging over her small frame (check), hair covered in a transparent rain-cap, despite clear skies (check), wrinkled, yellowy-brown nylons descending to tiny feet (check), small shoes, slightly off-green with blunt heels (check), purse dangling on her left arm, left hand in pocket (check). Hair grey. Skin jaundiced and creased. Glasses thick. Eye colour: undetermined from this angle (check, check, check, check).

Still staring at the old woman, Frank asks, "Are you my mother?" his voice loud in the small shelter.

The old woman doesn't acknowledge the query. She remains motionless, unchanged, cemented in her stance.

"Are you my mother? Are you my mother?" Frank tries again. He shifts on the bench, shimmying in the old woman's direction discreetly.

Through a whisper he calls to her, "Old woman. Old woman. Come out, come out wherever you are. Are you my mother? Are you my mother?"

Still she doesn't respond. Leaning carefully forward, with deliberate old-aged slowness, the woman reaches down and pulls her bag of produce closer to her small feet. A second later, she checks the straps of her off-green purse, making sure they are securely woven around her left arm.

Frank, still on the bench, tries again. "That Dr. Seuss book. Are you my mother? Are you my mother? You read it to your grandchildren, don't you?"

The woman, silent still, looks at Frank. She opens her mouth and begins to speak, her brittle lips dry, painted with bright red paste. Her mouth parts but no words come out. Franks stares at her yellow dentures, her purple tongue flapping in her tiny, crinkled mouth. He sees flashes from the back of her throat. He stands and peers into her mouth like a dentist. He watches a streamer of saliva run from her upper lip to her bottom lip. On her puny face he sees a mole covered with thick, black hair just to the left of her mouth, beside her sunken nose, below her tiny glasses. He reaches out to hold her face in his hands, trying to cup her small head in his palms. He can't get close to her; he can't touch her, he can't hear a word she says.

A second later, the bus crowds the curb and the old woman turns and leaves, her bag of produce clanging off her thin leg as she climbs the steps into the bus.

Frank, alone in the shelter, cries to himself, his tears spilling to the pavement. He tries to speak, but no words come. He reaches out with one hand to the departed bus, touching nothing. He leans forward, brushing his fallen tears away with his shoe, smearing them into the ground.

Around eleven o'clock, a middle-aged man walking a dog passes in front of Frank. The man stops, genuflects, and plucks the coin from the gutter. Frank, slouched on the bench in the shelter, raises his fingers to his lips and fumbles with his spittle, making idiotic baby sounds to himself.

Just past noon, the sun vanishes behind a dark bank of clouds. A woman rolls into the shelter, pushing a baby-buggy. She smiles at Frank and turns the buggy away from him, pointing it out the shelter's entrance. Frank stares at her, taking in her form. She is in her late twenties, her hair knotted on top of her head. She is dressed in tight aerobic clothing, a light jacket coming down just enough to cover her ass. Her legs are lean, meagre, muscular. Her breasts show slightly beneath the fabric of her thin jacket. Her face is colourful, vigorous, healthy. She could be a model in an advertisement plastered to the wall of a bus shelter, one of those lingerie models.

Silently, his eyes still on her, Frank digs one hand into his trouser pocket, nudging coins and keys, rubbing himself. The woman ignores him, her eyes set forward into the street. She transfers her weight uncomfortably from foot to foot. She pushes and pulls on the buggy, soothing the child within.

"Rats," Franks says, his eyes closed, his right arm out, pointing past the woman.

She doesn't respond. Keeps her eyes glued on the asphalt outside the bus shelter.

"Rats," Frank tries again, one eye coming open.

Again, he is ignored.

From his seated position, Frank yells at the woman, desperate to rouse her attention. "RATS, I SAID. BIG NORWAY RATS STRAIGHT FROM FUCKING NORWAY. RIGHT THERE BY YOUR FEET."

The woman, her face flushing, remains silent. She breathes deeply, trying to stay calm. She rocks the child in front of her, her hands tensed into fists, wrapped around the handles of the buggy, veins pronounced beneath her skin. The baby begins to sputter and weep.

Frank, his hands folded in his lap, falls silent, his head turned away from the woman and the noises coming from the carriage.

A minute later, the bus appears and the woman gathers up the child and the buggy and struggles into the coach. Frank, from his bench, offers help, but is given no reply.


One-thirty, Frank is alone in the shelter. A bus stops and lets out a strong, pressurized gasp. The driver, dressed in a light brown cardigan sweater on top of a cream-coloured shirt and tan trousers, marches towards Frank. He waves a finger in the air. He takes off his sunglasses, folding them into the breast pocket of his shirt. He enters the shelter and leans towards Frank. He mutters something about harassing passengers. He says something about radioing the police. He points towards the map on the wall, asking Frank where he is headed in the city. He warns Frank about being in the shelter any longer. He says that if Frank is still in the shelter on his next run, the police will be summoned. The driver reiterates, saying he doesn't actually have the authority per se, but, to clarify, to be absolutely clear, to be crystal-clear, he just has to radio his supervisor and she can send a cop over. Easy as pie. Easy as you please. No skin off my ass, he says. Just doing my job. Just following rules, guidelines. Just minding the needs of the passengers; those good people who pay their fares, ride the bus, keep public transport viable, put their money in the box, keep the bus company in business, keep me in a job.

His lecture complete, the driver strides away from Frank. The bus roars back to life, diesel fumes clouding the air outside the shelter.


Ten minutes later, about twenty minutes before two o'clock in the afternoon, Frank stands and walks out of the bus shelter. He crosses the street to a telephone booth. He draws a quarter from his pocket and calls a cab. He steps away from the booth and waits on the corner. He toes debris collected in the gutter at his feet. He watches pedestrians crossing with the light, cars creeping around the corner, a cyclist dodging past a nosing bumper.

A minute later the cab appears. Without a word, Frank climbs in and leans forward. It's the same driver. He looks drowsy. He looks wary of Frank. A Rolling Stones song plays on the radio, something about someone being under someone else's thumb.

Frank points at the meter. He whistles to himself and leans forward, kissing the cabbie on the cheek. "Take me home," he says in his ear, the hair by the driver's ear greasy, unwashed.

The driver, exhausted, confused and lonely, ignores Frank, wiping the kiss from his face.

Frank, silent as a mouse, shuffles back in the seat. He stares out the window. He thinks about asking the driver how his shift is going, how his day is unravelling. But he doesn't. He reaches into his pocket and withdraws all his remaining change, tossing it forward into the front seat. The driver peers momentarily at the coins, before turning up the volume on the radio. Frank smiles and snaps his fingers along with the music. He doesn't know the words. He opens his mouth and pretends to sing, strange clucking noises rising from his throat.

# BLUEBERRIES AND RED WINE

I'm making blueberry pancakes for forty. I found a large bag of frozen blueberries under some carrots and green beans in the walk-in freezer. I dumped the blueberries into the pancake batter, churning the yellow substance into a thick, pasty lather, streaking it with flecks of colour from the berries.

The grill is fired up and greased with butter. I dip into the batter with a ladle and make circles on the grill. Behind me, out by the benches and the tables, Ken and Jerome rouse the men, women, and children from sleep. It's six-thirty in the morning. Breakfast is served at seven o'clock sharp. Those who don't wake up won't get breakfast and won't be admitted to the shelter tomorrow night. By eight o'clock breakfast will have been served; I will have done the dishes and cleaned the kitchen; and the people who come to the shelter will be released onto the street, well fed, ready to take on the world.

The blueberries cause a bit of a stir. Arthur and Edina say something about having breakfast at the Royal Connaught Hotel when I serve them the pancakes. Then they say something about being royalty themselves: King Arthur and Queen Edina. I ask them where their kingdom is; a stupid grin on my face, my hands caked in batter. They laugh together and say the Balmoral Tavern is their kingdom, that they would fight to the death to protect it from space invaders, from the Nazis, from Attila the Hun. After this, Arthur asks for extra syrup. I take the sticky bottle and hold it over his two pancakes. I can smell him from this distance: the familiar stench of stale piss, stale booze, and street grime. He smiles, thanks me, and turns away, telling Edina that she should have asked for extra syrup, too, that I am not such a bad guy after all.

Only Henry complains about the blueberries. At the counter, he accuses me of trying to poison him with experimental dye. Henry turns to Ken and tells him that they did this to him during the war. Overhearing the conversation, I want to ask Henry, "which war?"

Henry is in his mid-forties. Every night he comes in with a new complaint. Usually it's about the noise. Last month he was barred from the shelter for two weeks after spitting on a woman's face for snoring. He stood over her and slowly drooled a pool of saliva onto her face and hair. She didn't wake up, even when Stan, another regular, confronted Henry, shoving him against a wall and then kicking him in the nuts. I thought for a second that the sleeping woman covered in Henry's spit was dead. But she woke eventually, oblivious to the commotion. Both Henry and Stan were tossed out into the street at three o'clock in the morning. When Henry appeared the next night, Ken and Jerome wouldn't let him in. Henry's face was cut and bruised. His knuckles were purple and swollen. He banged on the door and spat on the window, before eventually skulking away.

Blueberries, Henry explains to Ken this morning, are used to identify liars and enemies of the state. He says that prisoners during the war were force-fed blueberries every morning. Those prisoners whose skin on their stomachs turned blue were considered liars and enemies of the state. They were promptly executed. Henry keeps repeating the phrase "liars and enemies of the state." He tells all this to Ken and then tosses his tray at a wall, slathering the grey bricks with broken pancake.

I want to scream at Henry, tell him that the blueberries are my idea of a treat, a break from the usual grey food; that everyone else is happy to eat something different for a change. I want to jump out from behind the counter that separates the kitchen from the cafeteria and grab Henry by the collar and yell in his pockmarked face at one hundred and fifty decibels, "WHICH FUCKING WAR WERE YOU IN?" But I don't. I just stand and lean on the counter, watching Ken and Jerome shuttle Henry out to the street. The sight has become all too common. Henry protests, swearing and pointing back at me, his brownish-yellow fingers wriggling in the air. Once outside, he turns and kicks the door and then gobs on the window. All the others in the shelter ignore him. They seem happy with blueberry pancakes.

At eight-thirty, Ken, Jerome, and I sit in the Sunrise Restaurant with Bill. Bill works the kitchen on the nights I don't. There was a brief staff meeting after work and now the four of us have gone out for breakfast. We never eat the food at the shelter. Even though I cook it, and know the food is good, we prefer the breakfast specials at the Sunrise.

Bill is blowing smoke, listening to Ken relay the story of Henry. Ken, his voice high and squeaky, tells Bill that Henry threw his pancakes against the wall, and then whipped out his dick and pissed on the floor, before Ken threw him out. I look at Jerome. He smokes a thin cigar and doesn't say a word. We both know that Ken is lying about the pissing bit. Ken has a tendency to dramatize events, to stretch the truth and present a rendition of events at the shelter that seems more grandiose, more exciting. I think about the blueberries. I imagine force-feeding blueberries to Ken and then lifting up his shirt to see if his pot-belly turns blue.

Bill, too, knows that Ken is full of shit, but he indulges

him. Bill is aware of Ken's past and feels he owes him something. Ken is an ex-con, as is Jerome. They both did time in various facilities in and around Kingston. They are now reformed. The church helped save them. In prison, Ken tried to kill himself three or four times. Bill knows all this because his uncle was a chaplain in the Kingston Pen. Bill's uncle helped Ken go straight when he got out of prison. He got Ken the job at the shelter through a local connection. Now Ken reads the Bible day and night. He often comes into the kitchen at four o'clock in the morning and throws a quote at me when everyone is sleeping and Jerome is out walking the silent city streets. I like the time between three and five because I can get some reading done. Ken always asks me what I'm reading and then makes a sour face when he hears my reply, before holding the Bible up, waving it in my face. "I've got other copies," he says, offering me the Good Book. I tell him, invariably, that I have a Bible at home, that I often read the Old Testament, preferring the Book of Leviticus. Ken never knows what to say to this. He usually mutters something about Numbers and shuffles off, his nose jammed into the faded, thin pages.

Jerome stands and says that he's leaving. It's his turn to pay for breakfast. Ken reminds him of this as Jerome puts on his coat. Jerome always wears a grey trench coat to work on top of a three-piece suit. The people at the shelter say he looks like a lawyer, a bad lawyer. Jerome is trying too hard to be something he is not. He is the night supervisor of the drop-in programme at the shelter but he spends most of the night walking the streets, or flipping through magazines at the twenty-four hour bookstore around the corner. He hates the job. He hates Ken. The two of them have almost come to blows on several occasions. Jerome seems ambivalent towards me, but he doesn't trust me because I read books in the kitchen. Bill he likes because of Bill's uncle.

Jerome doesn't speak as he tosses a ten and a five on the table, the five smearing into a spilled puddle of coffee next to Ken's cup. Ken starts to say something but then bites his tongue. Bill smokes and looks past Ken out into the street. I take the damp bill, wipe it, and place it on top of the ten. Ken thinks this is funny for some reason and squeals in his nervous twitter, trying to get Bill's attention. But no one acknowledges Ken's noise.

A minute later the waitress appears and scoops up the money, muttering something under her breath. She doesn't come back with change.

Out on the street I hang around with Bill. It's quarter past nine on a Wednesday morning in the middle of May. Already it seems to be warmer than it should be for this time of year. I'm exhausted coming off my shift but I'm also wide awake, having had four or five cups of coffee with my French toast. Ken has left. He lives in Toronto and rides the bus into Hamilton five days a week to work at the shelter. Ken lives in a halfway house with a bunch of other ex-cons. Jerome lives up on the mountain somewhere and drives a Jeep to work. According to Bill, Jerome did time for embezzling funds from the insurance company that he worked for. He was also, supposedly, connected to some of Hamilton's more prominent crime families. Ken, on the other hand, was a small timer: a thief and a cheat. He only got hooked up with Jerome because of the Church, because of Bill's uncle. Now, on the outside, it's Ken who still quotes the scriptures. Jerome is more interested in three-piece suits, cigars, cars, and magazines.

Bill and I decide to go back to his place on King Street. He's working on some new paintings and wants my opinion. Bill is an artist of relative significance in the city. He's had a few shows, sold a few paintings. He also plays drums in a bizarre funk-folk band called The Battling Tops. We have known each other since high school. He helped me get the job at the shelter. We alternate shifts each week—one week I work two, he works five, and visa versa. I claim to be a writer, also of relative significance. I have had a few stories printed in small literary magazines and last year I published a collection of my work in chapbook form. I do occasional readings in Hess Village. Bill comes to hear me read and comments on my work. I watch him drum with The

Battling Tops and offer my opinion on his paintings. Together, we help each other to believe that our artistic pursuits are viable, meaningful.


On the way to Bill's place on King Street we bump into Henry coming out of Christopher's Restaurant. He greets us like long, lost brothers, throwing one arm around Bill and smiling at me. He can't remember our names. He's drunk and gregarious, apparently having forgotten the blueberry incident. He asks us where we're going on such a fine night. I want to tell him that it's about nine-thirty on a Wednesday morning but I don't. We make small talk with Henry for a minute outside the restaurant, hoping to put him at ease, before continuing on to Bill's apartment. But Henry seems to want to hang around. He's talking up a storm. He tells us about a stripper from Quebec working at the Foxes Den that he met last night. He makes up some type of French sounding name and rounds his hands in front of his chest, indicating the size of her breasts. He bends at the waist and then slaps himself on the ass. He says he's meeting her later for drinks at the Bayview Tavern, a bar where local prostitutes often work. Bill nods and smokes his cigarette. I listen to Henry, tempted to punch holes in his story. It seems odd to me that a stripper from Quebec—good enough to work the Foxes Den—would be slumming at the Bayview as well. But I stay mute. I remember how Henry burst into a rage over the blueberries and I wouldn't favour such an incident on the street.

Finally, growing impatient, Bill invites Henry back to his apartment. Henry nods his head like a broken puppet and grins madly. He asks Bill if he has anything to drink. I sigh behind the two of them. The last thing I want to do is hang out with Henry after coming down off my shift. The guy is fucking nuts and totally unpredictable. I was looking forward to spending an hour with Bill, winding down, discussing his paintings and perhaps my writing. But it's not going to happen this way.

Twenty minutes later the three of us are back at Bill's apartment. The walls are covered with paintings. Most have to do with one of two things: the naked female form or suicide. The colours are dark and the figures are emaciated and look diseased. We are drinking beer. Henry is pacing around the room maniacally, taking in all the paintings at once, blurring the images in his head. He is whistling and pointing as he spins. Beer spills from his bottle on to the paint-splattered floor. I'm sitting in the windowsill, drinking warm beer at ten o'clock in the morning, alternating between looking at Henry, the paintings, and the street outside the window. Bill is watching Henry spin out of control.

A minute later, Bill rolls a joint and lights it up, offering it to Henry. Henry stops twirling and whistling. He sucks on the joint as if it's a tit, keeping it to himself for too long. Finally, he passes it back to Bill. I finish my beer and walk past the two of them and open a bottle of red wine over by the stove. I take the wine back to the windowsill and drink straight from the bottle, occasionally spitting red saliva out the window, onto the street below.

Henry, splayed out on the floor now, begins to tell Bill about his sculptures. Henry says that he sculpts nude women and hung men, just like in Bill's paintings. He holds his hands out again, making the same obscene gesture he made when describing the French stripper's breasts. He laughs and rolls around on the floor, drunk and high in the mid-morning. Bill stares at him, curious with Henry's behaviour. I'm tired of Henry's behaviour. Tired of the lies. Tired of Henry's stunts. Tired of Henry.

Fifteen minutes later, the bottle of red wine almost empty, I stand and walk over to Henry. He's still going on about his sculptures. He says City Hall wants him to display one of his sculptures in Gore Park, behind the war memorial. He says the mayor stopped him in the street the other day and offered him ten thousand dollars to do the work. City Hall wants something new from Henry. Preferably something with enormous breasts, he says.

I've had enough. Finishing the last of the red wine, I tell

Henry to shut up. I tell him no one believes a word he says. I say he isn't a sculptor. I tell him his date with the stripper is bullshit. I then add that the bit about the blueberries—blue dye on his stomach, "liars and enemies of the state," and the war—is all a figment of Henry's wild imagination. I say all this and then toss the empty wine bottle into the sink. It crashes against a stack of filthy dishes. A few cockroaches flit away onto the counter beside the sink. Then I point at Henry and tell him to just shut up for once. I say that he has no business here, that Bill and I want to discuss the paintings intelligently, alone, without him. Henry, up from the floor now, just stands there, his hands folded in front of him like a child being scolded by an exhausted, irritated parent. Bill nods his head slowly and smokes a cigarette. He's high and doesn't say a word, doesn't support my argument, or refute it. I'm drunk and angry. Henry is high, drunk, and annoying. Nobody says anything further.

A minute later I feel like being sick and push past Henry, back over to the open window. My outburst has upset my stomach. Leaning forward, I puke a stream of red wine, beer, and French toast out into the street. It splashes on the sidewalk. A few people holler up at me. I wipe pink drool from my face and blunder towards the door to Bill's apartment. Henry laughs at me, saying I can't hold my liquor and something more about blueberries. I'm not sure but I think he uses the phrase "liars and enemies of the state" one last time. Bill just says that he'll call me later that night at work. He seems unbothered by all this. He smokes his cigarette and watches Henry scuttle around his apartment. I leave without closing the door behind me.

Out on the street I step past my vomit and stumble towards the bus-stops in Gore Park. It's eleven o'clock on a Wednesday morning. The sun is hammering down. I close my eyes, avoiding the glare coming up off the sidewalk. I'm nauseous, worn out, and drunk. I'm going home to sleep it off. I'm due at work again tonight at midnight.

# BLISS

"I'm just saying a good frying pan should last more than three months!"

"And how the hell would you know the first thing about frying pans?"

"I know. Believe me, I know. Look at this fuckin' thing. Do you really expect me to use this? Would you eat fresh fish that came out of this pan?" Tom holds the charred frying pan aloft, waving it like a broken banner.

"It's fuckin' useless. Covered in crap. Where'd you buy this piece of shit?"

Darla marches past Tom to the window, rearing her back. He starts in again.

"I'm just trying to get my stuff together tonight because Gus and Ernie will be round first thing in the morning to load up the van and I don't—"

Darla cuts Tom off, whirling around to face him.

"Gus and Ernie. Gus and Ernie. Gus and fuckin' Ernie!"

Tom recoils, lowering the frying pan to his hip.

"I'm sick of those fuckin' names. Everything's Gus and fuckin' Ernie!"

Darla waves her arms madly in the air, as if clearing the room of a foul odour.

"Yeah, Gus and Ernie," Tom says.

Darla interrupts again. "Those two sacks of shit are no use to no one. You spend more time with them than anybody else. They're milking you for your money. They let you pay for everything. You always do the driving . . ."

Tom steps towards Darla, worked-up once more.

"What the hell are you on about now?"

He still has the frying pan clenched in his left hand.

Darla says, "Those two dead-beats. Gus and fuckin' Ernie."

Darla's voice fades. She has nothing further to say about Tom's two best friends. She looks at him across the room standing there like an imbecile in his camouflage pants, white T-shirt, and bright orange hat; frying pan in one hand.

Tom tries to explain. "They're my best friends, Darla; I shouldn't have to tell you that. We do shit together. That's what's got you all pissed off."

"Who's pissed off? I don't give a fiddler's fuck what you do with those two piss-tanks. Go jerk each other off in the woods for all I care! Hunting your bloody messengers! It's them two leeching off you that I don't like."

Tom stares at her. He's confused for a second but lets Darla continue her verbal assault.

"Hockey tickets. Hockey pools. Pro-line tickets. 6-49. Beer on Thursday, Friday, Saturday night. Hunting trips. You end up paying for it all. They're like a couple of fuckin' kids taking you for all you're worth; you're just too thick to see the difference!"

Again Darla waves her hands through the air. She wishes she had a frying pan to support her argument. She scans the room quickly, grabbing a magazine off the coffee table. She balls it up as if she's about to smack a dog.

"What the fuck you gonna do with that?" Tom asks, still armed with the frying pan.

Darla circles the room, swatting at invisible flies, using up excess energy.

"I'm just sick of the sight of those two. Coming round here bumming for meals. They got jobs. They got paycheques. There's no reason why they can't pay for shit. What they don't got is wives at home to feed their fat asses . . . A pair of faggoty-assed momma's boys, the two of them . . . Dumb shits."

Darla is back at the window again, peering out on the street as if she's expecting company.

Tom shifts to the offensive.

"Oh, that's fuckin' nice talk, Darla. Fine fuckin' words for a lady to use."

His voice has the sarcastic lilt that eats at Darla, but she keeps her eyes on the street, blood boiling in her veins.

Tom continues. "We'd love to bring you along if that's what you're after. Cook and wash up and all."

He's smirking behind her back. He's waiting for her to lunge into another desperate diatribe.

But Darla resists. Summoning all her resolve, she keeps quiet, anticipating Tom's next blunder; waiting for him to say something ridiculous, something she can use against him.

"The problem being, Darla dear, that no one could cook up a thing on this cruddy frying pan! It's caked in shit. I don't know what you do in that kitchen, but there's no way we'll be able to use this fuckin' thing on the trip!"

Darla has the magazine rolled up, the end pressed under her chin. She spins, extending her arm, pointing her prop at Tom. She thinks she has him where she wants him.

"That's just it! You won't be frying up no fish. You'll be lucky to remember to take along some fuckin' grease-burgers to cook! And I know who'll pay for 'em if you do remember. You, Tom! They make you pay for every goddamn thing!"

Darla is livid again, her eyes blazing like rifles.

"You won't catch any fish! You won't shoot any messengers, neither! Not with them two fucks in the woods with you. They'll be so pissed the whole time they'll scare all the little birdies away!"

She waves her magazine madly through the air, simulating the flight of birds, before continuing, "And I don't know why you'd eat them Jesus messengers. Bloody birds taste more like fish anyways. Cheap shit birds. No good for eating. Shit birds for shitheads."

Tom looks genuinely puzzled. Calmly, he takes one step towards her. "Darla dear, what the hell are you on about now?"

Darla glares at him, her left arm still flapping slightly, as if she wants to fly off into the horizon.

Neither of them speak. They stand three metres apart, looking at each other as if for the first time, as if they have just stumbled out of the wilderness and come across strange, unrecognizable beings. Their eyes have that glazed look, that look of total astonishment and muddied confusion that only married couples share. That look that says: "I have absolutely no fucking clue what you're on about now." Which in Tom's case is pretty much true.

He places the frying pan gently on the coffee table before removing the fluorescent beacon from his head. He tosses the hat over by his gear in the hallway: boots, duffel bag, tackle box, fishing rod, and a pair of rifles wait for tomorrow's trip.

Darla scrutinizes Tom's every move, eager to pounce on his next remark.

Tom, rubbing his chin in a condescending fashion, turns to Darla once more.

"Messengers?"

Darla looks at him, slightly weakened at the knees.

Tom says it again. "Messengers."

He says the word as if he's talking about bicycle couriers, or receptionists poised over memo pads. He feigns confusion. He knows what Darla is trying to say, but taunts her nonetheless.

"You think we're going out into the bush to shoot bike couriers, or maybe secretaries?" A smile spans his face.

Darla looks hurt and perplexed. The magazine slides from her grasp, plopping onto the carpet at her bare feet.

"You don't have a fuckin' clue; that's always been your problem," Tom says. He's over by his gear now, sifting through it.

"Messengers."

Darla opens her mouth as if willing to retract her statement. She tries to remember the correct name of the bird, thinking it will help her plead her case.

"We hunt ducks, not *mergansers*, Darla. Get it fuckin' right for once."

He squats and puts on his boots, then straightens, rolling up the shirt sleeve on his left arm, fixing a digital watch to his wrist. He laughs lightly: audible ridicule aimed at his wife, and then rummages through the duffel bag once more.

Darla forgets about the name of the bird. She centres her gaze upon her husband pluming his fishing and hunting gear in the hallway. This is the man she married—this man dressed like an overweight militia boy poised for a week in the woods with a couple of useless drunks who take him for everything he's got; this man who never has a kind word for her; who, when he speaks, either speaks in anger or derision, barking orders or demeaning her; who hasn't offered a simple gesture of kindness towards her in months, probably years; who has focused all his attention on two drunken louts: hunting, fishing, playing hockey, drinking, traipsing through strip clubs like a pack of adolescents. This is the man she is stuck with.

Darla, barely able to hold herself upright, looks over at Tom. He's made two trips to the van. Half his gear is packed, ready to go.

"You're leaving tonight."

It's a statement, not a question.

Tom slings the duffel bag over his shoulder.

"Messengers. Messenger pigeons, maybe? Wait'll I tell Gus and Ernie about this one. Fuck sakes."

He laughs in her face.

"We'll see if we can't bring back a couple of messengers for you to cook up. But you'll have to have a pretty big pot!" Tom roars with laughter, then steps out of the house.

Darla doesn't budge when she hears the van door slam shut on the street.

"Go have your fun," she says to the empty room, and slumps down on the couch, the crumpled magazine on the floor by her feet.

After a second or two and a deep exhale, Darla reaches for the converter and the TV Guide on the coffee table. She looks over to the mantel, checking the time on the clock. She turns the machine on. The screen pops, fizzles slightly, and then catches, illuminating the room. Darla scans the pages of the TV Guide, then tosses it aside, clanging it off the discarded frying pan. The rest of the night she sits in a funk, meaningless images blurring blandly before her.

# FLOWERS, OH SUCH BEAUTIFUL FLOWERS

Sarah carried flowers at my wedding eighteen years ago. She was nine years old then, a dozen years younger than her sister Stephanie, my bride. Sarah, then, was clearly a child, compared to my twenty-six years.

Now she is naked in bed beside me—Sarah, that is, not Stephanie—the smooth, tanned calf of her left leg peering out from beneath the rumpled sheets on her bed. Her hair, cropped short, is as black as it was then. She hasn't messed with the colour. Her eyes are closed and peaceful, mascara blotted in the corners that point towards her lightly, freckled nose. She is beautiful at rest. But not quite angelic.

I cannot disturb her. I slip quietly out of bed and walk naked across her carpeted bedroom, heading down the short hallway to the washroom. I lean forward over the toilet and piss into the bright blue bowl. I flip my penis from side to side by rotating my hips, shaking out the last drops of urine. I tug idly at my dick. The scent of rubber clings to my hand. I smile into the mirror above the sink. I love the smell of latex in the morning.

The last time I saw Sarah—before all of this started up—was when I was still married to her older sister. That was six years ago, half a year before Stephanie and I finally divorced.

Thanksgiving. Sarah was in her second year of university. She decided to stay home and go to school in town. She seemed timid, then. She called me Jake, following her older sister's example. Both claimed I bore some weird resemblance to an uncle I had never met, or never would. He died a year before I came into the scene.

Anyway, Thanksgiving. That was our last public appearance at a family gathering as husband and wife. In all honesty, Stephanie and I were already separated. But nobody knew. It was a marriage that was doomed from the start. We were incompatible on virtually every level, including sexually. Stephanie wasn't interested in indulging my admittedly lurid preoccupations. She wasn't adventurous, not at all imaginative. This is my claim, now, anyway. Maybe she was more sensible and secure. Maybe I was too caught up in diversions, too eager to sweep troubles under the carpet, behind the door, wherever. Getting drunk, muttering nasty things in her ears. Stephanie wouldn't put up with it. Who can blame her, really? I wouldn't have put up with it. I didn't put up with it. I turned elsewhere. Stephanie just turned away—completely—and wanted nothing to do with me. I don't blame her. I'm the first to admit that I'm a narcissistic prick; always have been.

The plan at the time was to drop the bomb between Thanksgiving and Christmas, halfway between, some time around Remembrance Day when people were accustomed to hearing explosions, when everyone would be feeling sober, sombre, and nostalgic. But we didn't make it that far. And I was to blame.

Later that October, Stephanie's mom showed up unannounced on Hallowe'en to hand out candy. She found me stripped to my shorts, three days' growth splotching my chin, nuzzled up on the living room floor next to Wanda from the office, Patsy Cline blaring from the stereo. Stephanie's mom let herself in when she didn't get an answer at the door. When she saw Wanda and me, she shrieked like a skewered runt and dropped her candied apples. Wanda laughed when I ran out onto the porch and waved stupidly to my ex-mother-in-law swerving away down the street in her navy blue town car. Christ, what a disaster.

Stephanie was the one to leave the house. The memories, she said, were too much for her to bear. Memories of what, I wondered? She couldn't and wouldn't explain. And, as usual, I couldn't read her mind.

I think Stephanie was staying at a hotel downtown, but I wasn't sure. Not that her mom stuck around long enough to ask me that Hallowe'en. Needless to say, after the events of October 31, I wouldn't be welcome at Christmas dinner several weeks later.

Anyway, back to Thanksgiving. That was one god-awful, uncomfortable evening. I ate like a beast to dodge conversation. Stephanie's relatives were notorious for dragging the truth out of anyone they broke bread with. I remember a dozen times pointing at my working jaw with my fork, imploring with my eyes that I would love to respond to the inquisition but, goddammit, my mouth was too stuffed with stuffing to utter a peep. Fortunately, Sarah had some pimply-faced punk from her philosophy class with her who was a larger, more vulnerable target than me. The horde worked him over so thoroughly with intrusive questions that he was never seen again. I think Sarah preferred it that way. She did nothing to ward off the prying aunts and uncles and left poor what's-his-name to fend for himself.

Anyway, Thanksgiving. That night, that Monday night in early October, I looked at Sarah differently. With my mouth full of mashed potato I gazed at her, realizing for the first time how much Sarah looked like her older sister. Almost exactly like Stephanie did on the day that I married her. Sarah was no longer a flower girl. She was no longer an annoying adolescent. She was a young woman, a university student, fashionably dressed in the grunge look of the day, sex screaming from every pore beneath the layers of grubby flannel. I wanted to slather her in cranberry jelly and lick purple goo from her glistening body. I wanted to baste her in turkey juice and slide in and out of every orifice on her tender body. I wanted to eat pumpkin pie off her flat stomach, blindfolded, with my arms tied behind my back. All of this ran through my head in seconds as my soon-to-be-ex-wife played dolefully with the cold squash on her dinner plate. Christ, when I think about it now, I realize I have so much to be thankful for.


Five years later, my marriage a murky memory, I literally bumped into Sarah at another festive occasion. I was bringing in the New Year with a bunch of drunks from work in a small bar in the west end. I was good and pissed by the time the hour was perpendicular. Quick to engage in the New Year's tradition, I darted from colleague to colleague, sliding my tongue down the warm throats of women I had no previous interest in, one hand wrapped around my drink, the other kneading their doughy thighs. I was in a veritable reverie. I felt Roman, debauched. I giggled drunkenly and growled like an animal. I murmured unmentionable things in scented ears. I rubbed my crotch against sequins and nylon, stumbling from woman to woman, moving from co-workers on to co-workers' wives, to complete strangers, and finally to Sarah. I thought I was hallucinating, overcome by so much perfume and lipstick that my brain had seized-up. I groped for reality, sliding one arm around Sarah's slender waist, drawing my ex-sister-in-law into my lair. She didn't need to be coerced. Sarah came at me with equal vigour, a lioness in heat, something straight off the Discovery Channel. We were locked in a pre-coital kiss within seconds. She purred as I tightened my grip, hissed when I sucked on her ear. I drew my nails down her spine as she slipped her left hand into my front trouser pocket, testing my resilience.

An hour later we fucked like wild dogs. Sarah had my pants open in the foyer of her apartment building. I entered her in the elevator around the fourth floor and carried her

straddling me down the hallway to Apartment 608. We finished on an area rug in her living room, jackets still on,
dishevelled and crumpled around our shoulders.

Since then, it has been a regular thing. The sex, that is.
A purely physical relationship. Very physical. The kind of
relationship you see portrayed in Hollywood movies. No
diversions. No dates. No dreary commitments of any kind.
Just abrupt telephone calls, cab rides, and unfettered fucking.

It crosses my mind every once and again that at one time
Sarah and I were technically related. In-laws, however. Not
blood-relatives. My ex-wife's younger sister, to reiterate.
Illegal? Incestuous? No, I don't think so. Sleazy, certainly.
But sleazy is clearly not beyond me. Chalk it up to a mid-life
crisis. A twenty-seven-year-old woman. A forty-four-year-old
man. A tired script to be sure.


Back in her bedroom, Sarah has shifted her position. She
has drawn the blankets up around her, her leg no longer jut-
ting out. She still looks quite beautiful but won't be disap-
pointed when she wakes to find me gone.

I dress beside the bed. The belt on my jeans rattles and
Sarah stirs, mumbles something and rolls away. Past her
pillow-shrouded head, a bedside table supports a collection
of small-framed photographs: Sarah and a bunch of friends
white-water rafting on the Ottawa River; Sarah and her
mom and dad at her graduation from McMaster; Sarah as a
child with a dog long since passed-on. And speaking of
passed-on, Sarah and Stephanie arm-in-arm in front of a
Christmas tree. A Christmas after I dropped out of the picture. Stephanie looks good in the shot—I will concede this.
She looks radiant, some burden eased.

I turn away swiftly, refusing nostalgia and retreat from
Sarah. On the floor, strewn by the bed, lie her black underwear and an empty, bright-red condom package. I stoop
down, pocket the panties, leave the refuse where it lies and
stalk quietly away, leaving my flower girl to her morning
slumber.

21 DAYS

I pass Gina, the landlord, on the stairs that lead up to my apartment. She gives me a half-smile and I grunt at her, my bicycle slung over my right shoulder, pressed against the wall. Behind me, I hear Gina push open the building's front door and step out onto the street, before I continue up to my apartment. Gina never says much, aside from, "It's the first, I'm here for the rent." This is fine with me. I'm not interested in forming a relationship of any sort with her, with my landlord.

At the top of the stairs I take my bike down off my shoulder and push a key through the door. To my left I catch a glimpse of something white on my neighbour's door, about three metres further down the hall. Randy lives next door. With my door ajar, I lean my bike in the frame and then step towards Randy's place. Affixed to the door is a sheet of legal-sized paper, photocopied and blurry. An eviction notice. I lean closer. The notice states that Randy has twenty-one days to clear out of the property. After twenty-one days legal

action will ensue if Randy has not vacated Apartment D at
462 Charlton Avenue. I lean closer still and note that Randy
has not paid this month's rent, despite numerous requests
from Gina. He has also been truant providing the rent on
time on several previous occasions. Gina's name is printed
once and then scrawled at the bottom of the sheet. From the
other side of the door I hear Randy's stereo: The Rolling
Stones' *Prodigal Son* from their *Beggar's Banquet* album, by
the sounds of it.

Two days later, when I come home from work, the sheet has
been removed from Randy's door. I can hear music coming
from Randy's apartment so I step over and knock. Randy
comes to the door dressed in faded jeans, holed at the knees,
and a thin, black, rock 'n roll T-shirt. His eyes are glassy, his
face grubby, his hands tawny, a smoke glowing between the
fingers of his trembling left hand.

"Hey," he says, parting the door, leaning lazily against its
frame.

I peer at him for a moment, assessing his mood.

"I saw Gina here a couple of days ago. And the notice."

Randy looks at me through eyes reduced to tiny slivers
and sucks on his cigarette.

"She didn't say a word to me. And then I saw the notice.
What a bitch. Everything all right?"

Randy steps back, his socked feet sliding across the hardwood. He doesn't say a word. I can hear the Stones on the
stereo behind him. I can also smell something strange coming from his apartment, like spilled gas, something industrial.

"It's not the first time," Randy says, finally.

I think about offering to help, asking if there is anything
I can do. And then I remember that Randy owes me thirty
dollars. I loan him money from time to time, five bucks here
and there to tide him over until he gets his next welfare
cheque. Given the notice, I am sceptical whether I will see
the cash this time around. I also wouldn't put it past Randy
to ask to borrow a month's rent. He wanted me to drive him

to Niagara Falls a few weeks ago to see his brother who promised to lend him money. Randy said he would give me ten bucks for gas. He was serious. It's at least a two-hour drive there and back and he thought ten bucks would cover it. I had to come up with a good excuse to discourage him. I said something about the car not running well. He countered, asking if he could borrow my bike to peddle down Highway 8, all the way to the Falls. That idea just seemed ridiculous.

I step back from Randy's door. "Well, let me know if you need a hand with anything." It's a fairly generic offer. Randy looks at me blankly, the comment not registering. I almost said, "If you need a hand moving," but from the look on Randy's face he doesn't appear to be contemplating a move. He mumbles something while dragging on his smoke and eases shut the door.

I realize a week later that I haven't heard the Stones for several days. Any time of day, if Randy is home, I can stand silently in my hallway and hear their familiar choruses resonating through the wall. In the corridor, outside my door, the music is always clearer. I have caught myself on several occasions standing in the corridor, flipping through my mail, absently humming along to *You Can't Always Get What You Want* or *Paint It Black*.

I realize as well that Randy has not taken up my "if you need a hand with anything" offer, which is odd. He usually knocks on my door once every three or four days to ask to borrow money, to use my phone, or to get some sugar for his tea. More often than not he is just very bored and wants a few minutes of conversation. I make a mental note to knock on Randy's door to see what's up if I still haven't heard anything from him over the next couple of days.

Days later, still no word from Randy. I sort of forgot about him, being busy at work, tired, grumpy for no particular reason.

Returning from work, I bump into Hugo outside the building. Hugo is locking his ten-speed to a pole. A twelve of Molson Canadian rests on the pavement beside him. Hugo is a friend of Randy's with whom I am vaguely familiar. I'm not crazy about him. Whenever Hugo visits, the Stones get louder, to the point where I lie in bed and can't read or sleep because of the din. I've tried earplugs, but found them uncomfortable.

I grunt at Hugo and he smiles.

"How's Randy? Haven't seen much of him lately."

Hugo picks up the case of beer and follows me to the front door of the apartment building. I let him in with my key.

"He's got himself in a bit of a situation, man," Hugo says as we pass through the door.

I hate it when Hugo ends every utterance with "man."

"Yeah, I saw the notice."

Hugo looks at me. "Then you know the score, man."

I want to say that I don't know the "score," again slightly perturbed by the "man" appendage. What I do know is that Randy is supposed to clear out in ten days or so, nothing more convoluted than this, despite Hugo's inference. But I just nod my head and step towards my door.

Hugo, the case of beer lodged under his left arm, raps on Randy's door with his right hand. Then he turns to face me.

"Drop over later for a beer, man."

I almost say, "Sure thing, man," getting all caught up in it, but just nod my head instead and stand stupidly outside my door. A few seconds later Randy appears and lets Hugo in. He looks me over for a moment without a word. Then they disappear into Apartment D without a sound, not a single Mick Jagger lyric or Keith Richards guitar lick coming from the flat.

My curiosity gets the better of me some time after nine o'clock. I can hear Hugo and Randy laughing on the other side of the wall. I step out into the corridor and knock. Randy calls out "it's open" and more laughter follows, like

the unlocked door is absolutely the most hilarious circum-
stance imaginable. I let myself in and stroll into the living
room. Randy and Hugo are camped out on the only two
chairs in the room, surrounded by guttering candles. The
place reeks of pot. Randy points to an orange crate in the
corner. He tells me to dump out the contents and take a seat.
I do as Randy says, scattering car and skin magazines across
the floor. A case of beer sits open on the floor between Randy
and Hugo. The blinds on the windows are drawn, letting in
light from the streetlights outside. Hugo offers me a beer
and I grab one. The beer is warm, but tastes great nonetheless. Around the floor, empty potato chip and pretzel bags
are dispersed among about a dozen empty tins of baked
beans. Randy is absently tossing a Swiss Army knife in the
air, smiling at Hugo. He doesn't say much to me, and seems
unconcerned with my presence.

Randy and Hugo chortle between themselves, recollecting
days past, from about ten years ago. They volley stories back
and forth about various trips to Algonquin Park, talking
about the moose on the highway in May. The black flies.
Run-ins with bears. About how drunk they got on this or
that trip. Hugo recollects some girl he met in 1988—dubbing
her the "university chick"—who he had sex with in the
woods underneath a swath of tarpaulin. I just sit and drink
my beer. Randy and Hugo look over at me once in a while to
make sure that I'm amused by their anecdotes, yet general-
ly excluding me from the conversation.

After three beers I stand to leave. Even though I live next
door, I ask Randy if I can use his washroom. I am curious
about the dark, the candles, the strewn bean tins and chip
bags, and want to nose around. Randy nods, pointing down
the dim hallway.

I walk to the can, leaving the door open to permit myself
light to piss, and urinate into the toilet. Stepping away from
the sink, I catch a whiff of an odd, fishy smell. I turn towards
the tub. Three fishing poles and a tackle box are set inside
the tub in a shallow puddle of turbid water. I look into the
box. It contains nothing aside from the usual: lures, fishing

line, a knife, old Styrofoam containers caked in worm gunk. The poles, too, seem unremarkable. I turn away and think nothing further of it, slightly buzzed on the Canadian. I let myself out of the apartment, returning to my place without another word from Randy or Hugo.

Another bout of silence from next door finally breaks a few days later. I listen from my hallway as Randy bangs around in his apartment: a series of dull thuds, followed by a few sharp cracks. It sounds like he's whacking something against the floor, trying to break something. A couple of minutes later, the noise stops. I dismiss the disturbance and step into my kitchen to put on a pot of coffee.

Randy knocks on my door—for the first time in about two weeks—a minute later. I let him in. He looks worse than usual: gaunt, pale, slightly shrivelled, a dehydrated version of himself. His hands are shaking more than usual and there seems to be an odd, ashen substance congealing in the corners of his eyes.

"Hey," he grunts.

"Randy, what's up? Haven't heard from you in days. Everything alright?"

He looks past me, scanning my kitchen, before rubbing his eyes. He looks like he hasn't been exposed to artificial light in days.

I try to get his attention. "How's that business with Gina going? You getting it all sorted out?"

Randy looks back at me. He lifts a smoke to his pursed lips; his shaking hands on the verge of full-fledged trembling. "Oh, it's all coming together, man," he says, exhaling smoke in my direction. Again his eyes fall across my kitchen behind me.

"You got any wood? Maybe a saw?" Randy asks.

I wave smoke away from my face, then peer at him through the haze.

"Wood?"

Randy stares at me for a second, not responding.

"What the hell do you want with wood?"

Randy, simulating my gesture, fans a hand through the air as well. "Actually, forget about it, man. Don't worry about the wood. But how 'bout the saw?"

"No. No saw."

Behind me I can hear my coffee maker groaning, indicating the pot is full. I start to say something to Randy to chase him away but he seems ready to leave on his own.

"Sorry 'bout the noise," he says, and skirts away in his socked feet.

I hear the door to his apartment slam shut a few seconds later.

Two days later, on a particularly cold, October morning, I reach to close the window to my bedroom and spot Randy behind the building. He's bundled up in layers of flannel: two lumber jackets billowing out at his hips. He's carrying a bucket in each hand. Curious, I watch him approach the house behind our apartment building. Gazing around, he squats beside an outdoor faucet on the side of our neighbour's house. He fills both buckets with water and then crosses the yard back to our building. From my window, making sure he doesn't see me, I watch Randy struggle, water sloshing over the lips of the buckets, wetting the knees of his jeans.

Later that afternoon, returning from the pharmacy around the corner via the alleyway beside the building, I catch a glimpse of Randy at his window. He's rummaging around with the blinds. I step behind a hydro pole to obscure myself and observe his behaviour. The blinds flap and bang against the window before Randy pushes open the window, his head sprouting out for a second. He peers from left to right, checking, it seems, if the coast is clear. I stay huddled behind the pole and watch as Randy's head disappears and is replaced by his dick. In the middle of a Saturday afternoon Randy pisses out his bedroom window, his urine splashing audibly on the pavement outside the building. He zips up when he's done and then slams shut the window. I skirt out from behind the pole and head back into the building, confounded by Randy's antics.

Later that same day, I run into Randy in the alleyway. I'm putting my garbage out, tossing a plastic bag onto the heap of rubbish. Randy appears from behind a garage on my left, his arms bundled with scraps of something unrecognizable in the dark. He starts to dash away but I call out to him. Cautiously, Randy steps out into the light cast from a street-light behind us.

"What's up?" I ask, rubbing my hands together, the night air cold.

Randy, shaking fully, like he's overcome with palsy, steps towards me.

"Is that wood?" I ask.

He doesn't say anything. He stands motionless, uncomfortable with my inquisition.

"You need a hand with all that?"

Still wordless, Randy steps towards me, a wicked grin suddenly creeping across his face. He drops the faggot onto the alleyway's pavement. He points at the lot, picking up some of the larger pieces and starts to head back to the front of the building. I gather up what looks like shredded fragments of a particleboard bookcase and follow him.

Inside the building, Randy kicks open the door to his apartment. I follow still, my arms loaded with woody debris.

Since my last visit, the interior of Randy's place has changed. The two chairs that he and Hugo were sitting on have disappeared. Gone, too, are the orange crate and magazines. In the centre of the living room a small tent has been erected: an army-green, two-person, Canadian Tire type of tent. A Coleman stove sits against one wall. About half a dozen cases of Canadian are stacked neatly in one corner. The chip bags and bean tins have been cleaned up. Hanging from the light fixture above us, three plastic bags bulging with food dangle about two metres above the floor—speaking of which, the hardwood is littered with scraps of wood and leaves.

Without a word, I follow Randy past the tent, still laden with the wood from the alleyway. Behind the tent, Randy stops and turns to face me.

"Just pile it up there," he says pointing to a mishmash of table legs, twigs, and cardboard.

He steps to the right and drops his pile in the furthest corner of the room, beneath an open window. My arms free of wood, I look over at Randy. He begins to assemble his collection of wood in a large metal bucket. Above the bucket a battered stretch of pipe runs up to the window. It has been crudely rigged with wire and unravelled coat hangers: a bizarre ventilation system. Beside the bucket, a container of lighter fluid rests on the floor. I watch as Randy squats over the bucket, arranging the wood just so, before dousing it with lighter fluid. Drawing a packet of matches from the breast pocket of his exterior lumber jacket, he then sets the detritus ablaze. I step back instinctively, a swell of fire and heat coming up from the floor. Randy, smiling, rubs his hands over the fire. He is still hunkered on the floor.

"Don't tell Gina," he says in a croaking voice from his squat. "And make yourself useful. Grab us a couple of beers."

He points to an open case next to the tent in the middle of the living room.

The beer is colder than it was the last time I was invited over for a drink, this October having been unseasonably cool. Randy and I sup contentedly from the lager sitting cross-legged on the floor, a few metres from the fire. With the pot of refuse flaming, he starts to explain. I haven't asked for an explanation, but Randy is determined to come clean.

For two hours I sit and listen to Randy's life story, all of it directed at me to explain the campsite appearance of his living room. Randy, in great detail, recounts his past over the fire. He tells me about his uneventful childhood, his dull home life in the midst of a disintegrating family, the years of banal schooling that led nowhere. He tells me about various dreary jobs that followed: roofer, garbage-man, a six-month stint in a mushroom processing factory, window-washer. He explains how he lost his last job—going back seven years—because of his alcoholism. His last day of work he was found passed-out on a scaffold beside an office tower, pissed to the gills, twenty-three storeys above the pavement. After this, Randy recounts his time in hospital. After temporarily giving up drinking, he became chronically depressed and was eventually diagnosed as schizophrenic at the age of twenty-seven. Two years of sporadic institutionalization followed, shuffled between various facilities. A social worker eventually reintroduced him to the outside world, finding Randy an apartment, this apartment: Apartment D at 462 Charlton Avenue.

Randy tells me he has lived here almost five years. He has nowhere else to go. He is estranged from his crumbling family. He has no friends apart from Hugo. And he is behind on the rent. Because of this, he has taken matters into his own hands. Without heat, hydro, and running water, he has decided to camp in the apartment until he can afford to pay Gina. If this doesn't work, the next step, he says, is to barricade himself within the property.

I have nothing to say when Randy concludes his history. I have been drinking his beer, listening patiently to his explanation, occasionally gazing around at the strange interior of the apartment. The living room looks and smells exactly like a campsite. All that's missing is a roof of stars overhead.

But despite Randy's account, I feel I should tell him that his plan is not right. His strategy is basically insane, his actions the actions of a man who is not well in the head. I want to tell him that Gina has a key. That she will arrive tomorrow and let herself in and demand that he clean up the mess and vacate the property. I want to tell Randy that he can't barricade himself in like a crazed, American hermit, armed to the hilt. It won't work. And even if it does work for a day or two, he can't endure the coming winter camped-out in his living room, eating beans, drinking beer, smoking cigarettes, pissing out the back window, burning whatever will burn. This all seems obvious to me, but I don't say a word. I just thank Randy for his hospitality and leave, returning to my apartment next door.


The next day, three weeks to the day after the notice appeared on Randy's door, I pass Gina, the landlord, on the stairs that lead up to my apartment. She gives me a half-smile and I grunt at her, my bicycle slung over my right shoulder, pressed against the wall. Behind me, I hear Gina push open the building's front door and step out onto the street, before I continue up to my apartment. Gina never says much, aside from, "It's the first, I'm here for the rent." This is fine with me. I'm not interested in forming a relationship of any sort with her, with my landlord.

At the top of the stairs, I take my bike down off my shoulder and push a key through the door. With my door ajar, I guide my bike through the frame and then step inside. I throw my keys towards the table in the hallway. They clang on the floor. I look around, my eyes adjusting to the light. My apartment is completely empty, all of the contents, all of my worldly possessions, gone. Standing alone in the empty space, I can hear the Stones coming from next door. Leaning against the wall in the hallway, I hear laughter mixed with the music. I stand motionless, rubbing my hands together. I am chilled, suddenly. I breathe deeply and step into the empty living room. I smell a strangely familiar odour wafting through the hollow space that is my apartment: something like burnt wood.